Marked By His Alpha

Nesting Ever After

Jena Wade

Copyright © 2025 by Jena Wade

All rights reserved. This copy is intended for the original purchaser of this book ONLY. No part of this book may be reproduced, scanned, or distributed in any printed or electronic form without prior written permission from the author. Please do not participate in or encourage piracy of copyrighted materials in violation of the author's rights. Purchase only authorized editions.

Image/art disclaimer: Licensed material is being used for illustrative purposes only. Any person depicted in the licensed material is a model.

Published in the United States of America

This book is a work of fiction. While reference might be made to actual historical events or existing locations, the names, characters, places and incidents are either the product of the author's imagination or are used fictitiously, and any resemblance to actual persons, living or dead, business establishments, events, or locales is entirely coincidental.

NO AI TRAINING: Without in any way limiting the author's exclusive rights under copyright, any use of this publication to "train" generative artificial intelligence (AI) technologies to generate text is expressly prohibited. The author reserves all rights to license uses of this work for generative AI training and development of machine learning language models.
www.thejenawade.com

Warning

This book contains sexually explicit scenes and adult language and may be considered offensive to some readers. Jena Wade's books are for sale to adults ONLY, as defined by the laws of the country in which you made your purchase. Please store your files wisely, where they cannot be accessed by under-aged readers.

Contents

1. Chapter 1 — 1
2. Chapter 2 — 6
3. Chapter 3 — 13
4. Chapter 4 — 20
5. Chapter 5 — 26
6. Chapter 6 — 32
7. Chapter 7 — 38
8. Chapter 8 — 45
9. Chapter 9 — 51
10. Chapter 10 — 57
11. Chapter 11 — 64
12. Chapter 12 — 70
13. Chapter 13 — 76
14. Chapter 14 — 83

15. Chapter 15	90
16. Chapter 16	95
17. Chapter 17	101
18. Chapter 18	107
19. Chapter 19	113
20. Epilogue	119
21. Bonus Epilogue	124
Next In Series	128
Also By Jena Wade	130
About Jena Wade	138

Chapter 1

RAPHAEL

"Do you know where you will go?" my brother asked.

"No, that's the point of an adventure. I don't have a set route."

"So you're just going to pick a direction and go?"

"Exactly."

I had my cell phone squished between my ear and my shoulder while I stuffed the last of my belongings into my duffel bag. Folding was not a thing I attempted, even with my nicest clothes. I didn't have much. I had sold most of the items in my apartment; the rest I left for whomever the new tenant would be. Everything I needed, I had packed into a few suitcases and a duffel bag, which would be tossed into the backseat of my truck as I headed off to wherever I landed.

"I just think that you should have a better plan. What are you going to do for work? How are you going to have money?" My brother's concern, though appreciated, wasn't necessary.

I let out a breath. "I have savings. I will get a job wherever I land. I'm just going to drive and see what feels right."

Brock scoffed, and I could almost picture him standing there with his hand on his hip, glaring at me in a way only a brother could.

"Listen, you're on your own adventure. You didn't have a perfect plan either. What are you so worried about me for?" I asked.

"Never mind me. This isn't about me. You're my brother. Of course, I worry about you. What does Nolan think?" Brock referred to our third and final brother.

"He wished me luck. He trusted that I would be just fine, like I trusted that you would be just fine when you set out on your own," I said. "I need to get out here. If my fated mate is out there, I want to find them—same as you."

"I know, but I just can't believe you don't have a plan. I at least have my truck." Brock ran a food truck.

"Well, I'm still a certified firefighter. Most stations are looking for people. If not, they always need EMTs, which I'm also qualified for. If that doesn't work, there's always construction or basically anything else." The nice thing about being a dragon among humans was I was stronger than most and had better stamina. There wasn't much work that I couldn't do. "I'll be fine, Brock, I promise. I appreciate that you care." More than he might even realize. Family was all that I had, and leaving my brothers was not easy. Now that our dragons had emerged, we each felt the pull of the world to go out and explore. For me, that pull was to find my fated. The omega that was designed for me and for me alone. I couldn't wait to find him and spoil him with beautiful shiny things until my dragon was happy.

"You'll stay in touch?"

"Absolutely. Once I find my fated, you'll be the first to know."

"Perfect. I really do wish you luck, Brother. I want you to find all the happiness in the world."

"And I you. And also Nolan."

After a bit more chit-chat, we hung up, and I slipped my phone into my back pocket. I took one last look around my apartment to make sure I hadn't forgotten anything. I was leaving quite a few things—a bed, linens, my couch, my TV—all things that I could replace when I got wherever I was going. Mostly, I had my clothes, a few pictures of my brothers and me, and hopes and dreams. Plus, my hoard.

At twenty-five, my dragon had finally emerged. All my life, I'd known that I had the beast lurking in there. Now he was here, and with his emergence came a desire for my mate. I could just shift and fly to wherever I was going, but of course, I would drive. Humans couldn't know about dragons.

I just wanted to find my fated. It was lonely without a mate to share my life with. Sure, I was young, but shifters tended to settle while they were young and start their families. That was what I wanted to do.

I threw my things in the back of my truck and backed out of my parking spot. When I told Brock that I really didn't know where I was going, I was not exaggerating. I was simply letting my heart lead me. It may seem crazy, but I had a feeling it would work.

So when I came to a stop sign, I simply turned in the direction that felt right. Right now, that meant getting onto the highway and heading east.

Where that would take me, I did not know.

With each mile that I traveled, the anticipation of what was to come bubbled within me. I'd only ever known the town in which my brothers and I lived.

I couldn't even fathom what was waiting out there for me. When I closed my eyes and let my dragon dream, it wasn't of another dragon or even another shifter. No, in my heart of hearts, I felt that my mate was human. A man who had devoted his life in service to others, though how, I didn't know.

I longed to learn more about him.

As the sun dipped below the horizon, the miles I had traveled caught up to me. I'd let my dragon lead me the entire day, but the beast within me didn't need rest like my human side did.

I pulled into a parking lot of a twenty-four-hour diner. I wasn't hungry, but I needed sleep. The seat leaned back just enough for me to be comfortable, despite my long legs. It wasn't the best of circumstances, but the impatience of my dragon was only allowing me enough time to rest my eyes, and then we'd be back on the road.

When I slept, I dreamt of a small town that felt like a home. Of a cozy home close enough to the town center that I could walk to work. Of a cute little backyard with a swing set for my dragonets. Their laughter echoed around me; wherever they played, it wasn't where I could see them. The dream was hazy, consisting more of feelings and impressions rather than actual images.

"Raphael!" a voice called in my dream. The voice was melodious. A soothing sound that settled my dragon and made him purr. But when I turned, I couldn't see who was there. I knew it was my mate, but they were out of reach.

They were close, though. Wherever I was heading, it was in the right direction.

I awoke a few hours later, rested enough that I could continue my journey.

At least my dragon seemed amiable enough to allow me to eat. I grabbed a quick meal from the diner and then was on my way again, heading east like my dragon insisted.

Towns passed by and I paid them no mind. Until I came to a sign that read "Willowdale: The county's coziest town." Weird flex, but okay.

My dragon rumbled their delight, and my foot hit the gas. The engine roared and my speedometer jumped a notch. Whatever Willowdale was, that was where I needed to be.

My dragon insisted, and I wasn't questioning it.

Chapter 2

LUCA

I was four months into living in Willowdale, and I still couldn't get over how weird it was. In a nutshell, this place was goofy as fuck. Oh, it lived up to its designation as the coziest town. Someone designed the place straight out of a fairytale.

Main Street featured small shops, a bakery, a coffee shop, and the cutest library you ever saw. There was even a bookstore and a place that sold local handmade items from artisans in the area. Each storefront had a unique sign, and the buildings were clean and cared for. Locals gathered outside and chit-chatted about the weather.

Everyone was nice—more than nice. They smiled when they saw me, engaged me in conversation. Though I had only been here a short while, I knew most everyone's name. When I walked into a store or encountered someone on the street, they either knew me or knew about me. Like I was some sort of oddity. Sometimes, it just felt like everyone knew something that I didn't. It seemed that everyone I met had lived in this little town their entire life. I was the only transplant, except for a few who had married lifetime residents.

Was that odd? Probably.

But Willowdale was just so darn cozy and fun and nice. I couldn't leave it—plus, I needed the job. Because I was a paramedic with almost every possible specialization, I easily secured a position on their medical services team. I knew that I was sought after for my skills. Thankfully, the workplace was very well-managed, and I enjoyed it.

I had a schedule of three days on, three days off—three days of twelve-hour shifts, then three days without. Depending on the events of my shift, it was either incredibly boring or insanely busy. I loved it. I'd always known that I wanted to be a paramedic or a nurse. Once I made up my mind, nothing could stop me.

I was enjoying the last of my three days off. I had spent most of that time catching up on sleep, reading a few books, cleaning my apartment—generally being bored. Today, I needed to get out of the house.

My first stop: the coffee shop.

When I walked in the door, it was as if everyone there quieted down and looked at me. This was one of the many quirks of the place. It seemed like whenever I walked into a place, everyone grew quiet, like they had just been talking about me or about something I couldn't know about. But there was nothing to really say about me. I didn't do anything that would illicit any gossip. I was boring.

"Hi, Luca!" Michelle called. She was the manager of the coffee shop and worked the morning shift. "You looking for some coffee?"

"Of course," I said.

Bernice, the owner of the bakery, smiled at me. She stood on the customer side of the counter.

"What's on special today?" I asked.

"For you? Whatever you want. For everyone else? I felt like making pie."

"Pie sounds good," I said. "A little sugary for this early in the morning, but that's all right."

Michelle filled me a cup of coffee, adding a splash of creamer like she knew I liked, then slid over a plate with a slice of apple pie on it.

"Today your day off?" Bernice asked.

"It is," I said. "Back on schedule tomorrow at seven."

She nodded. "Well, if no one's told you about it, I suppose I'll be the first one."

I took a sip of my coffee, intrigued.

"A week from Sunday is the Midnight Maze Run. It tends to be an interesting event. The young boys like to compete for who can get up the Shadowpeak trail the fastest. You're bound to get plenty of sprained ankles—potentially a search-and-rescue."

"Fantastic," I said. "That trail isn't even dangerous, though?" I had been on a few hikes near the town. National forest and wildlife reserve surrounded the town. The trails were relatively tame as long as you stayed on them.

She chuckled. "Kids will be kids, I suppose."

"Yes, we were all young and dumb once. Thanks for the heads-up."

Michelle snorted. "Yeah, kids. As if there aren't just as many grown adults running the trail."

"Really?" I asked.

"Unfortunately. It's a tradition. It'll be fine, though. We don't get many serious injuries."

Still. It seemed like a silly thing to do if people were just going to get hurt.

"You settling in okay? Everything good? Normal?" Bernice asked. She searched my face as if looking for any sign that something was amiss.

I smiled kindly. "I love it here," I said. "Everyone's great."

Her brows rose in surprise. "Really? That's fantastic. You haven't had any issues with people treating you different? Or any local wildlife run-ins? Wolves or maybe bears?"

"No," I said. Not sure how I could be treated differently. I wasn't unlike many other residents. The place seemed to be a mix of different races and genders. Perhaps she was worried because I was gay? Still, I had seen more than one pride flag being flown. Jordan, the owner of the bookstore, was non-binary, and as far as I could tell, everyone treated them the same as everyone else.

As for the wildlife, I had seen plenty of tracks—a crazy amount, really. But never any of them in the flesh.

This conversation, like many others I'd had in this place, turned odd quickly.

"We're happy to have you here, Luca. You just let A— Tyler know if anything is amiss, all right?"

"Of course." That was the advice that I got from a lot of people: *Go to Tyler if you have any issues.* When I first arrived, I asked if Tyler was the mayor, and someone had laughed.

"Suppose you could call him that. It's fitting. In fact, when you meet him, call him Mayor," they had said that to me, and I just shrugged it off.

Still, as quirky as this place was, I loved it here. It felt like home. There may have been a few things missing—namely, a lack of alphas I was interested in pursuing—but still, I liked it.

I sat down at a booth and sipped my coffee. After a few minutes, the door chimed and my friend's voice filled the air.

"Michelle, dearest, I need your strongest coffee, love, pretty please." Theo's gaze caught mine, and he squealed. "Luca! You didn't tell me you were here!"

From the day I arrived in town, Theo had adopted me, and I didn't know why, but I didn't hate it. He vibrated with life and positive energy and somehow decided that we were besties.

"I was going to text you once I got my coffee."

"Any exciting plans today? We should go shopping!"

I laughed. That seemed to be his solution for a lot of things. Not that I could complain. I enjoyed hanging out with him. "I need groceries."

He wrinkled his nose. "Well, food shopping is still shopping, so we can do that. Afterwards, want to come over to mine? That baking show has a new episode that came out while you were working the other day. I haven't watched it yet. I saved it just for you, boo."

I grinned. "Yeah. That would be fun."

Michelle set a massive cup of coffee down in front of Theo. He stared up at her with stars in his eyes. "Thank you, thank you. I was afraid I'd perish without this sustenance. But now that I have it, I can find the energy to keep going." He blew her a kiss.

Michelle laughed. "You're ridiculous, Theo. We were just telling Luca about the Midnight Maze run. Are you doing it this year, Theo?"

Theo nodded vigorously. "Yeah! I can't wait."

"You? You hate running. You didn't even want to do the fundraiser walk with me last month. I had to promise a lazy day and buy you a new blanket in order to convince you."

He shrugged. "The Maze run is different. It's... tradition."

"What's the purpose of it?" There had to be more significance than they were letting on.

Michelle and Theo exchanged a glance. "Um... It's just for fun. There's a superstition that whoever finishes first will find their ma— life partner next."

"Oh. Well, that's kind of fun." Weird, but fun. Not that I believed in any of that sort of thing, but traditions were always fun. And it fit in with the rest of this town's quirks.

"Should I do it?"

"No!" Theo shouted. Then he smiled, grasping my forearm. "We need you to be a medic, dearest. Lots of silly w— runners get hurt."

I was met with lots of nods.

Yup. Definitely another one of this town's weird quirks.

Chapter 3

RAPHAEL

I drove over five hundred miles, stopping only at a few different places—including the parking lot to rest my eyes for a few hours—before a sudden sense of rightness overcame me.

As I suspected, it was the town of Willowdale.

Now that I'd crossed the city limits into Willowdale, I could see it was true to its description. It was a cozy little town that had a handful of stoplights. The streets were bustling with small-town activities, and cute little shops and stores lined the streets.

Like I had for my entire journey, I let my dragon guide me, which had me turning down a side street, driving two blocks, and then parking in front of a one-story ranch house with white trim and deep green shutters. The landscaping out front was lush with green gardenia bushes that were in bloom.

My dragon rumbled his approval.

Someone lived here. It wasn't as if I could buy or rent the house, so why was my dragon sure that it was ours? Some days I wished the creature came with a manual. He had never steered me wrong before, and I trusted him. The least he could do was provide a map.

I could not, however, remain outside some person's house staring like a crazy person. I forced myself to put the truck back into drive and pull onto the street.

With my dragon content with the town, I needed to scope out a place to actually stay.

Then I came upon the fire station, which sat on the corner, directly across from the bakery and the emergency medical services station. The words *Firefighters Wanted* flashed on the digital sign out front.

It was fate, and I would not question it.

I pulled into a parking spot, got out, and stretched my legs. I had lost track of how long I had been driving that stretch, but it had been a while.

The garage door was open, giving me a clear view of the three bays. Two of which had tanker trucks, while the other had a small ladder truck. No one was running about, so it didn't seem as if they were actively going toward a call. The place scented of shifters—a wolf, a bear, maybe a few others. At least I wouldn't have to worry about hiding my dragon.

I paused a moment and drew in the scents.

There were many different shifters here, and no signs of humans at all, anywhere in the town.

Come to think of it, the entire town kind of *scented* of shifters.

Did any humans live here?

"Can I help you with something?" a voice called.

I turned to see a man—an alpha wolf by the scent of him—approaching. He wore a pair of bunker pants and a navy-blue t-shirt with the department logo on the chest. Based on the peppering of gray in his hair, he was in his early to mid-forties. Or perhaps he was just the type to go gray early.

I held out a hand for him to shake. "My name's Raphael," I said. "I just arrived in town and wanted to talk with someone about the position available."

He shook my hand slowly, his nostrils flaring. "Dragon?"

I nodded.

He whistled. "Don't see many of those."

"No, sir."

"Well, welcome to Willowdale. You'll fit in fine. I'm Tyler, the fire chief here, also pack Alpha."

My brow rose in surprise. Should I bare my neck? I had interacted with wolves before, but never the Alpha of the pack.

He chuckled. "Don't worry about formalities. I don't care about that sort of thing. You looking for a long-term position or just a short while?"

"Long-term. I... I think my mate is here. My dragon... It's hard to explain."

He clapped me on the shoulder. "Let me guess, your dragon led you here, and he wants to stay?"

I nodded.

"See? Not difficult to explain to all. Maybe humans wouldn't understand, but we do. Let me give you a tour of the station."

As he led me deeper into the building, I couldn't help but feel like I was stepping into the right chapter of my life.

"Clearly, this is the engine bay." He gestured toward the trucks. "We're a small town, so we really don't need much. Two tanker trucks and the small aerial engine. We also have two pickups, one I drive primarily and the other is used for search-and-rescue. The EMS garage is across the street. We work closely with them. Let me show you the fun stuff."

We passed by lockers and cubbies with enough turnout gear for twenty people.

"How many firefighters do you all have?"

"Four full-time guys, plus me, but I'm more of a part-time chief, full-time Alpha. Then we have another fifteen that are volunteers. We service a lot of the rural area, as well as the whole town. And we help with neighboring towns when needed."

He led me into the office area.

"We'll come back here to do your paperwork, but I can show you the living area first. Do you need a place to stay or have you figured that out yet?"

"Not yet. I literally just pulled into town."

"I suspected as much. I would have heard if someone else had run into you. You can stay here until you find an apartment. It might not be ideal, but it's free."

"That will work. That won't cause any issues? I don't want to cause trouble with the crew for any special treatment."

Tyler waved a hand in the air. "Naw, we've all used the station as a temporary home once or twice. Hell, Sanjay's omega kicked his ass out of the house two years ago for a slight misunderstanding. He stayed here until he could beg for forgiveness." He winked. "But that's a story for a different day."

He kept walking. "This way to the common area."

As we walked, I took in the sense of family and camaraderie that filled the station. The walls were lined with past accolades and photos of the crew during downtime and town events.

The hall opened up into a large space that had a full kitchen straight ahead and a living room type space to the left. There was a large television, two plush couches, and a billiards table. A large table sat near the kitchen with a couple of half-finished puzzles and a chess board on it.

"The bedrooms and showers are on the upper level."

"Looks like you guys keep busy," I said.

"Hey, Alpha." Two broad-shouldered men came down the stairs. They stopped when they saw me.

"Dude, is that a dragon? Or... something else?" His nostrils flared, and he stepped closer.

"Dragon," I said.

"Guys, this is Raphael. He's going to be joining the team," Tyler said.

"Fantastic. I am so over these double shifts. I'm AJ." He held out his hand, and I shook it.

"I'm Levi. Resident bear shifter. Finally, I won't be the odd man out."

"You're still odd, Levi." AJ nudged his shoulder.

"Is the pack made up of multiple shifter types or..." I wasn't sure how to phrase the question without being offensive.

"Sort of. We have mostly bears and wolves in town, with a few other paranormal types around—witches and vampires and the like. The bears have their own den leader. I'm not the boss of everyone or anything like that."

"Bullshit. He's being modest. He leads the whole town. Don't let him tell you otherwise. Rory is the bear den leader. He lets Tyler have all the glory—and all the attention."

"Rory is the real brains behind this operation," AJ teased, nudging Levi with his elbow. "But seriously, we coexist pretty well. It's all about respecting each other's territories, you know?"

I smiled at their banter. The camaraderie flowed effortlessly between them, a stark contrast to the loneliness I had felt on the road. It felt good to be around other shifters who understood my nature without question.

"Nice to meet you guys," I said. "I just got into town, but I'm really feeling like I'm meant to be here."

Chapter 4

LUCA

One of the many things I loved about this small town was how closely the EMTs worked with the fire department. Sure, we had a rivalry, but it was friendly, and I was told that in the summer, there was a baseball game we played against one another to raise funds, but it was all in fun.

Tyler—the same Tyler who seemed to run the whole town—was also the fire chief. He wouldn't tolerate anyone being treated poorly.

We worked together regularly, which was why, when I was out of oxygen cylinders, I ran across the street hoping to get some of theirs. Our shipment wouldn't arrive until tomorrow, and we needed them to get through our shift. I snagged some of our leftover cookies from the order we had put in at the bakery this morning as a peace offering. I didn't need it, but that was another quirk of this town—everyone ate like they were a pack of ravenous wolves. Sometimes I wondered if the people were part animal. Theo sure ate like one, but he was somehow lean and fit.

I let myself into the main area that the guys used as a kitchen and common space, where they played video games or pool during their downtime. Since no one was actively on a run, the place was filled with the guys on duty.

"Hey, Luca, how can we help you?" Tyler asked. He was elbow-deep in dishes at the sink. Another thing I liked about this place—everyone pitched in.

I looked around, my gaze landing on a new guy.

He was tall and muscular—which was typical for guys on the fire department. He had a mane of dark hair that was a touch too long and curled around the collar of his navy-blue t-shirt. The five o'clock shadow on his face was just long enough to leave a beard burn. The very idea made my body heat. His bright blue eyes flashed as he turned to look at me. There was a magnetic quality to them, and I couldn't look away.

"Luca? You okay?" Tyler's amused voice snapped me out of my thoughts.

"I need oxygen," I said, snapping my gaze back to Tyler. "Cylinders. Oxygen cylinders."

Tyler snorted. "Sure thing. Just let me know how many you take. Or bring them back when your shipment comes in."

My gaze drifted back to the newcomer who was talking with Levi while they played pool.

"Are those for us or do you just carry a plate of cookies around for funsies?"

"Oh yeah." I set the platter on the counter. "I figured you couldn't say no if I came bearing gifts."

Tyler dried his hands on a towel, then reached for one of the cookies decorated like an ambulance. "You know we always got your back."

The newcomer laughed at something Levi said, and my mouth went dry. I was here for something, but I couldn't recall what it was, not when his rich laugh was drawing me toward him like we had an invisible lifeline drawing us together.

He couldn't seem to look away from me either.

Then a hand snapped in front of my face.

"Earth to Luca. Did you need something else, or did you just come to ogle the goods?"

My cheeks heated.

"No. I'm all set. I'll bring the cylinders back tomorrow, assuming we don't actually need them today."

"No worries. We know where to find you. But before you go—Raphael, come over here."

The man I couldn't stop staring at set down his pool cue and walked over.

He wore a pair of turnout pants and navy-blue department shirt like the rest of the guys. If we were running a "who wore it best" competition," he would win hands down. His eyes never left mine as he stalked across the room. My heart rate kicked up a notch, and I was sure I was going to tip the fire alarm because of the heat building in me.

"Luca, this is Raphael. Raphael, Luca. He just hired in, and thankfully, he was able to start immediately because Levi was going on his third shift in a row. And you know how he gets."

I chuckled. "It's nice to meet you," I said, holding out my hand.

He grasped it and shook. A little bolt of electricity shot up my arm, straight to my groin. This was ridiculous. I was not the type to objectify every alpha I came across, but there was something about this one.

"Are you new in town? I mean, obviously, you must be. I haven't seen you here before—not that I know everyone, but I mean, if you're a firefighter and you hadn't been working here before, you must be new, right?"

Tyler's brow shot up, and he looked between the two of us. His grin widened.

"I'm new," Raphael said. "Just arrived yesterday. Don't even have a place to stay yet. Thankfully, Tyler gave me a job."

"Oh, wow. Welcome. I, um—I work across the street." I jerked my thumb toward the window as if he didn't know which street I was referring to.

"Luca is one of the paramedics—one of the best—so you'll see him out there on scenes with us."

Raphael's eyes flashed as he smiled. "Great. I look forward to working with you," Raphael said. His eyes continued to bore into me as if he was really *seeing* me. They were the most beautiful shade of green—almost a deep emerald.

"I look forward to working with you, too."

"Raphael, why don't you be a gentleman and help Luca get the oxygen cylinders from the storeroom? Luca, we haven't given him the full tour of our supply area, so feel free to show him around."

"Okay," I said, still not looking away from the gorgeous man in front of me.

I wasn't the type to fawn over a man, even an alpha as amazing as him, yet I couldn't tear my gaze away. Also, my feet wouldn't move, like I was planted in cement and I needed the jaws of life to break me out.

"I'd really like that," Raphael said, lifting an elbow for me to slip my arm into. That got me moving. I slipped my arm into his, and the heat of his skin sent a shiver up my spine.

"Maybe you can show me around town later when our shifts are complete?" Raphael said. "I haven't been able to explore much, and I'd love a tour guide."

"I'd really like that," I said, licking my lips, my throat suddenly going dry.

"Great. I've heard this town has a few quirks."

I grinned. "It's quirky all right, but you get used to it."

As we made our way to the storage room, Raphael stayed close. The smoky scent of cologne hit my nostrils. I wanted to bury my face into his chest to inhale more of it. Damn alpha pheromones were getting to me.

"So, how did you pick Willowdale to land in?" I asked.

"It just… felt right. Like I was supposed to be here. Do you believe in fate, Luca?"

I stopped in front of the storeroom door. Raphael leaned against the frame, hovering over me with his height. I didn't feel crowded, though; in fact, I wanted to get closer to him.

I licked my lips. "Um, maybe? I don't really know."

He hummed and it was like his chest vibrated. "I'm beginning to think fate really knows what they're doing. After all, I'm here with you."

I sucked in a breath. This was insanity. But I wasn't running away, far from it. I was ready to leap into his arms, even though we had just met. Before I could do something entirely crazy, the radio I carried to alert me of any calls chirped. The spell was broken.

"I gotta go," I said. I ducked into the storeroom and grabbed what I needed, then made a mad dash across the street.

That was crazy, right? To be so drawn to someone so quickly. It had to be a fluke.

Next time I saw Raphael, I'd be normal.

Chapter 5

RAPHAEL

There was something about that omega human paramedic. My dragon purred with delight the moment we saw him. I knew it deep within my scales that he was the reason I was drawn to Willowdale.

Ever since he had stopped by the station, I hadn't been able to stop looking out the window, hoping to catch sight of him again. His scent lingered on me, and I was desperate to see him again in person. Maybe I'd make my way over there. I could make up some excuse to see him.

"Don't worry," Levi said, standing next to me at the kitchen sink, looking out the window across the street. "You'll see him again. We run into the EMTs all the time."

I didn't want to say the words out loud that had been ringing through my mind, but I couldn't stop myself. "I think he might be what I'm looking for."

"Well, good. Otherwise, all this obsessive pining for a man you interacted with for less than five minutes would be weird. But don't take him away from us, all right? We're rather fond of Luca around here."

"He's the only human I've encountered since I've been here. Granted, I haven't been here long, but the place doesn't *scent* of humans at all."

"They don't tend to stick around," Levi said. "And it's easier if they don't. We're not against having humans around—clearly, we love Luca—but it's just easier when they aren't sticking their noses in things. We like to be able to shift and run or talk about shifting. We don't have to worry about keeping our kids from shifting. When humans are around, we can't truly be ourselves. The only humans here are mates or Luca."

"So, is the hope that Luca will move on?" I asked.

"Not at all. We love him. He probably thinks we're all weird as hell, but we couldn't drive him out. We didn't even try. He's good people. He's special."

"He is indeed." My dragon rumbled at that. Luca was special because he was ours.

"Although, I think he's on to us. He thinks we're all a little weird—but he likes us anyway. Theo—he's my younger brother—is close friends with him."

If what I thought was true—if Luca was more important to me and my dragon than I could yet admit—then he would know our secret sooner or later. The rest of the town wouldn't have to worry about hiding themselves from him because he would learn about us.

Before I could dwell on that thought, the alarm sounded, and each of our pagers went off. The lights flashed, letting us all know that we had an emergency to tend to.

"We got a live one! Barn fire out on Turner Road. The old sheep barn. Get dressed," Tyler shouted. "Newbie, you're going on a run on your first day."

"I haven't even filled out my paperwork," I said. I wasn't actually concerned about that.

"We're not too worried. Besides, you're a dragon—you're fireproof, right?"

I laughed because, yes, I was indeed fireproof. That wasn't the only reason I went into this career. My dragon and I loved helping people, and this was one way we could help most. I could go into fires that others wouldn't dare.

Which was exactly why it was impossible for me to work on human crews. They never really understood how I could run into a burning building and get people out safely without a scratch, or how I always seemed to *know* exactly how a fire was going to spread or how it was going to grow.

I rode in the back of the truck as Tyler sped down the street with the sirens blaring. The ambulance was ahead of us, and I knew Luca was in there.

Once we arrived at the fire, the structure was engulfed in flames. The old wooden barn was secluded from the other building on site, but there were trees surrounding it. The crew set to work. It wasn't a raging fire, so I observed more than anything, helping wherever I was needed.

"Please!" a woman cried, panic thick in her voice. She went straight for Tyler. "Alpha. He's in there! He hasn't come out yet. I *know* he's in the barn!"

Tyler spoke into the walkie-talkie, alerting the ambulance crew and the rest of us.

"We have a person inside. Doug is in there. Fifty-year-old male. Susan, do you know where he might be in there? What was he working on?"

"I-I-I don't know. He might be in the pen getting it ready for the sheep we bought last week. They're supposed to arrive tomorrow. Oh god!" Tyler wrapped his arm around her shoulder.

"We'll find him. You're up, dragon," Tyler said.

I nodded. This was what I lived for. I wore my turnout gear, but it was mostly for show. I could walk in there without feeling the heat.

Levi and AJ flanked my sides. The two covered the entrance while I made my way inside. The flames licked the walls, igniting everything they came in contact with. If the man had been trapped in here the whole time, even with his shifter blood... we needed to act fast.

I'd never been in the barn before. Luckily the crew had. They gave directions to me through the system in our helmets. I walked carefully. With the smoke it was hard to see, and I didn't want to trip.

"Doug usually parks his tractor to your left," Levi's voice echoed through the headset that was wired inside my helmet. "It's possible he's there. Or perhaps the loft."

"I'll check the loft first. Before it comes down around us."

I quickly spotted the ladder leading up to the loft.

"I'm heading up," I said.

"Roger."

The climb wasn't graceful, but I made it quickly. The rickety ladder strained under my weight. My heart pounded. I wanted to find this person. He was a member of the town that I called home, and though I had never met him and I hadn't been in town long, I felt the connection.

Once I reached the top, I looked around. There were stacked bales of hay that smoked, moments away from igniting.

My eyes shifted to those of my dragon. I was able to focus through the haze, and that was when I spotted him.

There, in the corner of the loft, a man lay unconscious.

He had likely hurt himself trying to escape—or the smoke had gotten to him. I pulled off my mask and placed it over his nose. The wood beneath my feet creaked and groaned. Ash and soot danced in the air around me. The roof wasn't going to hold for much longer. I had a choice to make.

I shucked off my jacket and put it over Doug. He groaned as I lifted him in my arms. Just as I was considering how to get him down the ladder, the loft gave way.

The fire had eaten through its supports.

I kept the man in my arms as I hit the ground, taking the brunt of the fall myself to shield him. Debris landed on my shoulder, but I pushed it off and got to my feet.

Now I just needed to find my way out, even if that meant bursting through the wall.

"Raphael! Talk to us!"

Chapter 6

LUCA

I stood near the ambulance, out of the way but at the ready in case any of the firefighters needed me. I had all of my equipment ready. But since no one was inside, this would probably be an easy-peasy fire to deal with, and I likely wouldn't have any patients to care for—unless someone tripped over a hose and broke an arm, which I'd seen happen before. Not that the firefighter would admit they got injured in such a way.

Nevertheless, I was ready for anything.

I jumped when the barn began to fall. A haze of smoke and sparks flew, pushing a plume of dark smoke into the air. The heat rushed at me, and I felt it even from where I stood. There was a lot of shouting. Tyler was there, directing his staff around.

"Raphael's inside!" he shouted. "Clear a path! Let's get him out of there!"

I straightened at that. Raphael was inside that fire? No one had mentioned that there was someone inside.

Why my feet moved without me telling them to, I'd never know. Never would I imagine approaching Tyler in the middle of his work. He didn't need my pesky questions, yet I couldn't stop myself. I grabbed him by the arm.

"Raphael's inside? Why?"

His gaze softened when he saw me. "Doug was inside, according to his ma— wife. Raphael went in to find him. Levi and AJ were guiding him since they know the inside of the barn."

Just then, the side of the barn blew out, and a man—who had to be Raphael—stumbled out. He had someone cradled in his arms. His bare arms. His fireproof turnout jacket and helmet were not on him.

I sprang into action.

Everybody rushed to his side at once, and I set to work getting an oxygen tank. My crew moved with me. Without his coat and helmet on, we were looking at potential burns that would need attention fast, plus smoke inhalation.

"We're gonna need two ambulances," I said.

"Another one's on its way," someone responded.

Once I knew that Doug was being attended to, I went to Raphael's side. His skin was marred with fresh burns, although not nearly as bad as I would have assumed, considering he had just burst through a wall. Soot and dirt covered his face. His hair was singed.

"We need to get him to a hospital right now. Let's pack this thing up—alert Mercy General we're on our way."

"I'm fine," Raphael said, his voice without even a hint of raspiness to it—nothing like you would expect to hear after inhaling all that smoke.

I stilled. If I hadn't just seen that man burst through a burning building, I wouldn't believe it. No one came out of an inferno like that unscathed. Especially without his helmet on.

"Now is not the time to be macho, Raphael. Tell him, Tyler."

Tyler shrugged. "Nah, I think the burns seem like something we can treat here, and if he says he doesn't need a hospital—"

"Are you kidding me?" I shouted, my hands going to my hips as I stared them both down. "Seriously? He's badly injured! Even if he's sitting up and talking, he has to have smoke inhalation." I gestured to his arms, which were a mess of angry red burns and ash clinging to the seeping flesh. Blisters covered the back of his hands. "Look at him!"

"I have an oxygen cylinder." Raphael held it up. "Good thing you grabbed those."

I stared at him like he had lost his damn mind. He *had* to have lost his mind. He must be in shock. The pain from the burns alone had to be tormenting him.

"Did you hit your head in there?" I grabbed for my flashlight, ready to check his pupils.

"Luca, I swear to you, I am fine. I really appreciate your concern."

"There is no way I'm letting you just go back to work. These are second-degree burns at least. They need to be cleaned and treated—"

"He should definitely take the day off," Tyler said. "And based on the time, your shift's coming to an end soon. Luca, why don't you spend the evening with Raphael? Make sure he's all right?"

I opened my mouth to protest, but I could see that the two of them were not going to see reason.

I crossed my arms over my chest. "All right. But if I even get the hint that you might need a doctor, I am going to knock you out and take you there myself. And don't think I can't—I know exactly how to put you under and subdue you."

Raphael's eyes flashed, and the heat that coursed through my body had nothing to do with the inferno blazing just a few feet away.

"It's a deal," he said. His voice was like warm honey soothing my soul.

Oh, goodness.

I set to work getting his burns cleaned up, using cool water to wash away the soot and bits of debris that clung to his skin. The redness and swelling around the affected area dulled as I cleaned. The burns were not as severe as I originally thought. Somehow, they looked as if they were already healed.

"I suppose these aren't so bad, but really, Raphael. Of all the macho things to do."

Raphael chuckled, and it was almost as if I could feel the vibration against my skin. I forced myself to focus, to keep my eye on what I was doing or else I was going to end up messing up his bandages or forgetting to clean one of his many burns.

"It's my job, Luca. I promise I won't push my luck again."

"Please don't. I understand wanting to look good for your new boss, but you're no good to anyone dead. Goodness, you acted like you were fireproof out there."

"Can I get a water?" Raphael asked.

"Oh, of course." I stopped what I was doing and grabbed a bottle of water for him. His hands were freshly cleaned, and they looked too painful to use. "Um…" I unscrewed the cap and lifted the bottle to his lips.

Raphael drank.

Fuck. Now was not the time to be perving on the new guy in town.

Raphael's gaze met mine and a strange heat burned behind them. I licked my lips, suddenly feeling like I was the one with the burns.

"Try not to use your arms too much. They'll need to stay bandaged for the next twenty-four hours, then they get changed as needed after that. Okay?"

"Sure thing." Raphael smiled.

My face heated. "You've probably had burns you've had to treat before, so this is nothing new."

"Nope, but I like hearing it from you. Are you going to keep an eye on me the rest of the day?"

I nodded. "I guess I am."

The fire had dulled considerably now, and the second ambulance had already left with Doug to go to the hospital. I caught Tyler's eye, and he gave us the go-ahead to return to the station.

My partner, Charlie, and I put the gurney back into the ambulance.

"Ready?" I asked Raphael.

He nodded. "As I'll ever be."

Chapter 7

RAPHAEL

I didn't know whether to kick my new boss or kiss him. Sure, he had all but guaranteed that I would get more time with Luca—time to explore this explosive connection between us. But now I had to be around a human while my body rapidly healed all the burns that he had so intimately cared for.

Luca was going to get suspicious.

Thankfully, he was quick in his work to get them cleaned up and covered, because otherwise, he would notice that they were already starting to change. I willed my dragon back, forcing him not to speed up the healing process like I normally would. Already, the burn that had scorched our lungs and caused my voice to disappear had fixed itself. I knew it was a red flag for Luca that I somehow managed to escape the fire without any smoke inhalation issues, but he didn't seem to question it.

"I'm surprised you're not fussing about riding in the ambulance," Luca said.

I cleared my throat. "My desire to spend time with you outweighs my concern about how my new co-workers view me."

Luca chuckled. "I knew it was a macho thing. You firefighters are all the same. Once we get back to the station, I have some paperwork to do before I finish my shift, but you can rest if you'd like."

"I'd like that." I'd like any scenario where Luca was there with me. Sure, this wasn't the first date I had in mind, but I could work with it.

Luca sat with me the entire ride back to the station. Then he got me settled into one of their dorm rooms. They were slightly smaller than the dorms we had at the fire station, probably because they didn't do multi-day shifts like we did.

"I'll be back shortly," he said.

The building was quiet since everyone was still out fighting the fire. It would be hours before they all returned. If I slept, it was very likely that my dragon would heal all my burns, but it wasn't as if I could run around acting like everything was normal. Luca had lived in this town for months, and it had only taken a short amount of time with me here for us to risk exposing all of us.

I could at least hide them from him while they were bandaged. And he wasn't likely to want to unbandage for twenty-four hours so we didn't expose the open wounds to any germs. Only there weren't any open wounds anymore. My dragon had almost completely healed me. If we looked at the burns now, we'd see new pink skin.

After a while, Luca returned. He had a backpack slung over his shoulder.

"Did you get some rest?"

"Yes, I did." Sort of. I mostly spent the time worrying about how to explain to him what I was.

"Great." He handed me a bottle of water. "Make sure you're staying hydrated. I brought more bandages in case we need to change them. Maybe I should take a look, I feel like I rushed the cleaning while we were on site."

"They're fine," I said too quickly.

"I know. I know. We don't want to expose any germs unnecessarily. I'll leave them alone. Are you in any pain? I can't believe I didn't offer you any pain relief earlier. You just act so normal. I forget that you were injured."

I put my hand over Luca's. An electric jolt went through us at our touch, but I didn't pull away. "I promise I will let you know if I need anything. I realize I got thrust upon you by Tyler. Would you rather I not be here?" I asked.

He bit his lip, and I wanted to tug it free from his mouth.

"No. Not at all. I—I want you here. I want to hang out and keep an eye on you. Did you have other plans? I don't want to ruin your evening."

I shrugged. "I've got nothing going." I looked around the room. "We might be more comfortable at your home, though. Could we go there? I don't mean to invite myself—"

"You're more than welcome," Luca said. "Are you sure you don't mind moving again? You're supposed to be resting."

"Sounds like I'll be able to rest as soon as I get there." I flashed him my best grin, and Luca smiled back.

"Then let's go."

The drive to his house was short—not that I expected it to be long, considering how small the town was. But I was shocked when he pulled into the driveway of the very house that had caught my attention that first day in town. My dragon's intuition never ceased to amaze me. Of course he had led me to the home of the man I suspected was my mate.

"This is me," he said as he parked outside of the garage. "I can't fit my car in there. I've got way too much stuff, and I haven't sifted through all of it."

I swallowed thickly. "The house is adorable," I said. "Looks very cozy."

He chuckled. "Like the rest of the town, right? Yeah, when I saw this one for sale, I couldn't pass it up. Something about it just screamed *home*, you know?"

I nodded. I had that very same thought.

Inside the house was just as cozy as the outside. The scent of Luca was strong. My dragon rumbled his approval.

"Are you all right?" Luca asked.

"What? Yeah, I'm fine."

"Oh, I thought you sounded like you were in pain."

Luca put his things down and guided me toward the living room. It was located in the back of the house, with a large bay window that overlooked the yard. A white picket fence enclosed the yard, and a swing set sat in the center with a large sandbox.

"I'll get you something to drink, then we can relax."

"Sounds good. I'm fine, really. Almost as good as new."

Luca narrowed his eyes. "You may look fine, but you still need to take it easy."

I settled onto the sofa, sinking into the plush cushions.

Luca returned a moment later with a glass of water.

"Thank you for looking after me," I said. "I do appreciate it."

"Of course. I know what it's like to be new in this town."

"Yeah, and I'm staying at the fire station right now, I haven't found an apartment yet."

"Really? You moved here without a place to stay?"

I chuckled. "Yeah." I rubbed the back of my neck. I didn't want to seem like the type who didn't plan or think things through, but how did I explain to Luca that I was just trusting my dragon?

"My brothers and I all sort of left our hometown around the same time, each heading in a different direction."

"That's kind of fun. Are you close with your brothers?"

I nodded.

Luca settled next to me, tucking his feet under him and grabbing the blanket that rested on the back of the couch. "I don't have siblings, but I always wondered what it would be like."

"It's great. We're close. They've always supported me, and I support them. Even when we don't understand each other's decisions."

"Like moving to a random small town without a plan," he teased.

"Exactly like that. It was the right decision, though. I couldn't imagine being anywhere else right now."

Luca's eyes softened, and he leaned closer to me. He rested his head on his hand, with his elbow propped on the back of the couch. "I feel the same."

The pull between us was intense, and I kept my gaze focused on Luca. His eyes sparkled, and he looked at my lips. He sucked in a breath when my tongue darted out to wet my lips.

Just as I was about to close the distance between us, Luca's phone screeched loudly.

He bolted off the couch and went in search of his phone. "I'll be right back, and we'll figure out what we're doing for dinner, okay?"

I nodded. "Sounds good."

After a few moments, he came back. "That was Theo. He heard about the fire and wanted to see what I knew. He's a bit of a gossip. Why don't you try to rest a bit, okay?"

"I will. On one condition."

"Oh, and what's that?"

"Have dinner with me."

Luca's brow furrowed. "Oh, I'll make sure you get dinner. I'm not going to starve you."

"No. I mean, would you like to have dinner with me? Like a date. Tomorrow? Unless you have to work."

He grinned. "Not making it easy to say no, are you? I can't deny an injured man."

"Hey, if that's what it takes, I'll allow it. Is that a yes?"

Luca nodded. "Yes. I'll go out to dinner with you. And just so we're clear, I would have said yes even if you weren't injured."

Chapter 8

LUCA

"You are going to raise eyebrows," Theo said.

Ever since I moved in, people had introduced me to their nephews, their sons, their brothers. They weren't too pushy about it. After one introduction, they seemed to settle on the fact that sparks didn't fly, and nothing further came of it—which was nice. But in all my time here, I hadn't been on a date. Now I was going on a date with the other brand-new person in town.

As much as I didn't love people talking about me, I recognized that it wasn't malicious. Once the town found out Raphael had asked me on a date, it seemed that everyone was buzzing with excitement about it. It had only been thirty-six hours since he left my house after resting from his injuries.

"Okay, you're going to have to dish all the details," Theo said. He sat on my bed while I picked out my outfit for the night. I didn't have a ton to choose from. In fact, he had brought over a few dress shirts as options.

"There's nothing to dish," I said.

"Oh, there will be afterwards. And I got a sneak peek at that hunky drink of water that you landed. If you hadn't called dibs, I'd have been all over that."

I chuckled. "Dibs? I hardly called dibs."

"That's not what Tyler said," Theo sing-songed while he rocked on the bed, making silly faces.

I rolled my eyes. "Okay, so how's this look?" I wore a pair of dark skinny jeans with a kelly-green button-down. My leather ankle boots that I only pulled out for special occasions rounded out the outfit.

Theo gave me his nod of approval. "Undo the top button and play with your collar throughout the night. It'll draw attention to your neck. That drives guys like Raphael crazy."

"You haven't even met him."

"Well, it just drives guys crazy. You know how alphas are."

"Thanks," I said. "I'll take that into consideration."

The doorbell rang, and Theo launched himself out of my room and was down the hall faster than I could stop him.

I eyed the mess that was my bed and closet and decided I'd have to deal with that later. The last thing I wanted to do was leave Theo alone with Raphael.

"Well, hello there," Theo said when he opened the door.

"Hi," came Raphael's confused voice.

"Luca will just be a few minutes."

"I'm ready right now," I said, coming to Theo's side.

Theo rolled his eyes. "You're supposed to make them wait to prove that they can be patient. They have to work for it."

Raphael chuckled. "I feel as if I have already waited an eternity for this. I will not mind another few minutes if you need it."

From behind his back, he pulled a bouquet of flowers. As I reached out to grab them, he grasped my hand and kissed the back of it. A shiver ran down my spine.

"Thanks," I said. My voice came out breathless.

Theo fanned his face. "Oh, boy. Details later. You *have* to give them." He pushed his way past Raphael. "Have fun, you two! Don't do anything I wouldn't do!"

Raphael raised a brow as he looked at me. "I have a feeling that really doesn't limit any of our options."

"It really doesn't."

He chuckled and lifted an arm. "Shall we?"

"Yeah. Where do we plan on going?"

"Outside of town. I thought it might be nice to check out that Italian place over in Alma."

I let out a long breath. "Thank goodness. If we went to dinner here, everybody would be watching. Don't get me wrong—I love the food here, but we'd be under a microscope."

"That was what I suspected. And as much as I love this town, I would like time with just you."

I smiled. "I'd like that." I continued to hold on to him, and I couldn't resist leaning into him. The scent of him wrapped around me like a warm hug. I had the oddest urge to bury my face against his chest.

Raphael wore a long-sleeve shirt. He tugged his sleeves down his arms.

"Oh, goodness, I didn't even think about your burns! Are you—how are your hands so healed?" I grabbed his hand and inspected it, careful not to touch him too harshly. But it was amazing, as if no burn had ever occurred. The skin was smooth and unblemished, not a blister of burn anywhere.

"I'm a quick healer," he said.

"Quick? Raphael, this is insanity. This—this defies logic." I turned his hand over as if that was going to give me answers.

"I don't think the burns were as bad as they looked. Once they got cleaned up, it was mostly just blisters."

I was about to argue—after all, his reasoning was insane. Blisters took weeks to heal, no matter how bad they were. Anyone who'd had an irritation blister on their heel knew that. Plus, I was there, I saw him and tended to his burns right after they happened.

Still, when he laced his fingers into mine and his eyes on me, I melted. I couldn't put any more effort toward it.

"Shall we?" he said.

"Let's." My voice came out breathless and heady. Thank goodness I wasn't playing hard to get, because I would fail.

The conversation flowed easily on the drive to the restaurant. Raphael told me about his brothers, about growing up with the two of them. Meanwhile, I filled him in on some of the quirkier things I'd seen in town—including the reported sightings of many large animals, mostly bears and wolves.

"That's crazy," he said. "There weren't many bears where I came from."

"Me neither. I haven't seen any, but I've heard them when I am sitting on my deck at night. And there are always huge paw prints in the park. It's crazy how close to town they get. Tyler has assured me there's never been any attacks or anything though, so it's safe."

"What made you move from the big city to a small town?" Raphael asked.

"I love my job as a paramedic. I really do. I love being able to help, to be with people in their most hectic moments and be that level of calm. But the city was just burning me out too fast. Every shift was one tragedy after the next, and I needed a slower pace."

"That makes sense."

"Here, I can get to know the people that I'll be working with, which lends itself to its own dangers. It's very likely I will come upon an accident someday and know the people in the car. And that's never easy."

"I was called to a fire once. A friend I grew up with—his parents..."

My heart twisted for him. I couldn't imagine such a thing. I reached my hand over and grasped his. "That must have been awful."

"It was," he said. "Thankfully I was living close to my brothers at the time. They helped to ground me and encouraged me to talk to the department therapist. It helped."

"I'm glad."

We reached the restaurant, and Raphael parked. He was out of the truck and jogging around to my door before I could open it. I let him open it for me and help me out.

The restaurant was a charming little place, and the fresh scent of basil and tomato sauce wafted through the air.

"I'm never going to be able to pick a meal," I said.

"It's been a while since I've had good Italian, but I'm willing to share if you are." The fire in his eyes as he looked down at me sent a jolt through me. Every time I looked at him it made my skin tingle, and I had the oddest desire to get as close to him as possible—with no clothing between us. I'd never been so drawn to an alpha before, and my gut told me this was right. I wasn't going to question it.

"That sounds great."

Chapter 9

Raphael

Dinner could not have gone better.

We talked long after we had finished our meals. Our server was practically begging us to leave and give up the table. I left him a generous tip to make up for it.

I drove slowly on the way home since I had no desire to return to the fire station and my single lonely bed. Staying with Luca for as long as possible was my main priority. I was running out of excuses, though.

When I arrived at his house, I got out of the truck. I would absolutely walk him to his door like the gentleman that I was. With any luck, I may get a goodnight kiss and a promise of another date. Maybe we could even set a date for the next one.

I held his hand while I walked him to the door.

"I had a great time tonight," I said, feeling very much like a nervous teen awaiting their first kiss.

This would be my last first kiss. There would be no other man in my life except for Luca. He was my mate, my one and only. Just the anticipation of it was enough to bring my dragon roaring to the surface.

I stopped just outside his door and faced him. His eyes flashed like there was a heat behind them. Like a backdraft in action.

I didn't have time to prepare before he launched himself into my arms.

His lips landed on mine.

Time stood still.

I kept still.

Then he was moving, his tongue coaxing my mouth open, and I responded in kind. I moaned into his touch. His taste ignited the fire within my soul, like breathing life into me.

Luca put both hands on my shoulders, then jumped. His legs encircled my waist.

I gasped against his lips.

"Take me inside," he said. His voice was breathless and laced with seduction.

I didn't need to be told twice. I fumbled with the doorknob. He had locked it, but the flimsy metal was no match for my dragon's heat. With barely a touch, I melted the knob and the door swung open. The moment we entered the house, a warm rush of excitement coursed through me.

Luca tangled his fingers in my hair, not letting me go as our tongues danced. We explored each other's mouths while I stumbled through the house. He still had his legs around my waist, his chest against mine.

It took two tries before I found his bedroom. I could have focused and followed his scent, but I was too distracted with him clinging to me like a koala. His lips had moved from my lips to my neck, and his nails dug into my nape.

"Raphael," he gasped against my skin. "So warm. I need you inside me. I swear if you don't fill me with your cock, I'm going to implode."

I rumbled with pleasure, my dragon preening at the need in our mate's voice. "We can't have that."

I lowered us onto the bed, still covering his body with my own. "Mhmm, mate, you are going to have to let go of me for a moment so I can take these clothes off us."

"Rip them." His warm breath skated over my skin, then his lips were on mine again.

I hoped he wasn't too attached to these pants because I was going to follow his instructions exactly. I grabbed both sides of his collar and yanked until each of the buttons on his shirt gave way. Next, I grabbed the waistband of his jeans and tugged. The ripping of denim echoed through the room.

Luca gasped. "Holy shit. I didn't know that was possible."

While he was momentarily distracted, I removed my own clothes and tossed them to the floor next to his ruined ones.

"I'll buy you more," I said. I trailed kisses down his body until I found his thick cock. For a lithe human, his cock was long and girthy, making me wonder if he might consider topping sometime. Another time. Tonight was my turn.

Luca's hips bucked. "I'm burning for you, Raphael. Take me, please."

"Soon, my sweet."

His omega body was producing the slick I needed to ease the way for my cock. I pressed two fingers to his entrance and his body opened for me like a key fitting into a lock.

Luca spread his legs wider, and I pressed my fingers deeper, letting his body suck me in like he couldn't get enough of me. Soon, two fingers became three and he was thrashing on the bed. I curled my fingers inside him, pressing against the gland inside him that was sure to drive him wild.

Luca gripped my hair and pulled. "So fucking close. Give me your cock, please!"

"Mhmm, you beg so pretty for me," I said, pressing a kiss to his inner thigh. It quaked under my lips.

"Please, Raphael, please. I need you to fill me."

I let my fingers slip from his body, and he let out a whine.

I silenced him with a kiss. "Shhh, I'll take care of you," I murmured against his lips.

That settled him, and his legs spread wider for me.

My cock slid into his body like it belonged here. His channel embraced me, clenching against my shaft until I was blind with pleasure.

Luca's hips bucked, urging me deeper.

Every nerve in my body burned brighter than dragon fire, and my emerald scales erupted on my arms. My hips moved, each thrust sending waves of pleasure through me and into my mate. He clung to me, his nails digging into my back.

"Raphael, more. Please, more."

I would die to hear that word on my mate's lips. His begging would be my undoing.

I growled, the sound not at all like something a human would make, but hopefully Luca wouldn't notice. My pace quickened.

I sensed my orgasm and his, and I chased it. I wrapped my hand around his cock, appreciative of the size of him. He was a handful. I stroked him in time with my thrusts, and within in a moment, our orgasms shook through us. His cock erupted, sending ropey white spurts of cum between us.

My thrusts faltered as my release pulsed out of me. I filled his hole with my cum. HIs body clenched around me, even as my knot expanded, locking us together, pressing against his inner walls.

His eyes widened and his eyes rolled back. "Oh fuck!"

We stayed like that for a long moment. Our hearts pounding in sync, our breath catching.

Eventually, my knot released enough that I was able to slip out of him. By then he was blinking slowly, his eyes unfocused.

"Luca, are you with me?" I asked.

"Hmm. I'm good." He sighed and snuggled against me.

We were sticky. Slick and cum dripped down his legs and his cum cooled on my belly. A shower was in order, but it didn't seem as if he would get up anytime soon.

No matter. I could take care of him.

I slipped from the bed, reluctantly. I grabbed a towel and cleaned myself off, then returned to the bed and did the same for him.

For half a second, I debated crawling into the bed with him. He hadn't invited me to stay the night, but I'd rather have my scales plucked one by one before I'd leave my mate's side. I decided it was better to have him kick me out rather than leave on my own.

Clearly I made the right choice as I climbed into the bed and Luca snuggled closer to me. "Wake me up for round two," he whispered against my chest.

"You can count on it," I said.

Chapter 10

LUCA

Raphael and I needed to talk. Not in a bad way, but there were definitely things that were not adding up about him—his healing ability, his weird scales. The fact that his skin felt hotter than a furnace when he was buried deep in me last night.

Something wasn't right, and I had a feeling it had something to do with how weird this town was. There was a connection, but I didn't know what it was.

Raphael lay next to me, sleeping soundly. I leaned up on one elbow and gazed down at him. He didn't even look like he had a building fall on him just a few days ago. He was perfectly normal. The laugh lines around his lips were smooth while he slept. The scruff on his face had grown overnight, making me wonder if he ever considered having a longer beard if he wasn't a firefighter. Did he let it grow out when he was not on shift?

"Are you watching me sleep?" he asked. His eyes remained closed, and a small smile played at his lips.

"Yes," I replied. My hand trailed up his naked chest. Even now he burned hotter than a regular person. If I didn't know better, I'd think he had a fever.

"I have better things we could be doing." His eyes opened, flashing with desire. He reached for me, but I stopped him.

"We'll get to that *after* we talk."

He grimaced. "Right. Should we talk over coffee?"

"Am I going to need coffee for this conversation?"

He nodded. "If you're going to ask about the things I think you're going to ask about, coffee would be best."

"All right," I said. At least I wasn't blindsiding him. Which meant he likely knew what I was going to ask about and he had an explanation. Was it superhuman strength? Was he secretly Superman?

The two of us got out of bed, taking turns using the restroom. He pulled on the jeans he wore the night before, and I tried desperately not to get distracted by his nakedness.

My clothes from the night before were in tatters on the floor. Good thing I hadn't borrowed any from Theo.

Thankfully, I had a coffee pot that worked quickly, and within a few moments, the two of us had coffee in front of us.

"You are not human, are you?" I asked. Best just to rip this band-aid off quickly. I wanted answers.

He took a deep breath. "No, I'm not. At least not entirely."

Oh shit. I was right. I hated being right. "What about everybody else in this town?"

He winced. "They aren't human either."

"What—am I the only human in town?" Was that why everyone was weird around me and why they went quiet when I walked into a room?

"You're the only human not mated to a shifter."

I swore it was like a record scratch in my brain. "Wait. What? What is a shifter?"

"Why don't I start at the beginning?" he said. "You can ask questions as they come up. I just want to say that I should have told you this before last night. I'm very sorry about that. It's just—"

"Raphael, if you had tried to have this conversation with me last night, I wouldn't have let you. I'm pretty sure I attacked you." More like I couldn't keep my hands off him. Something wild had come over me last night. I wasn't complaining. It had been worth it.

He chuckled. "Yeah, you were a bit overtaken."

That was being polite about it. I wasn't ashamed of my behavior. It had been amazing and so incredibly worth it, even if I had looked like a crazy person.

Raphael ran his hand through his hair and down his face. "I'm a dragon. My brothers and I are all dragons. We came from one clutch—kind of like triplets. All three of us were hatched at the same time."

"Wait—you were hatched? Like, from eggs?"

His face strained and he nodded.

"Am *I* going to have eggs?" I wasn't dumb. I was an omega, he was an alpha. We had sex. Multiple times. We used protection each time after the first one, but hot damn, it had been an intense night. My face heated just thinking about it.

Raphael winced. "I mean... maybe? When I turned twenty-five just a few weeks ago, my dragon came out for the first time."

"I bet he's beautiful." I reached my hand across and squeezed his. In the throes of passion the previous night, I swore I could picture his dragon. At the time, I'd thought I'd just gone mad with lust, but perhaps it was something else?

"I'll show him to you soon. My brothers and I each left our hometown in search of our mates. We all wanted to find our omegas, or in Brock's case, his Alpha. I came here because I was drawn to this town. Drawn to you."

"What is everyone else in town?" They couldn't be human.

"Your friend Theo is a bear."

"What? I would have guessed wolf." Theo had that wolfish behavior about him. Then again, what experience did I have with it?

"He's a bear. Tyler is a wolf. Most everyone is either a wolf or a bear, and Tyler is their Alpha."

I nodded. "That's why everyone goes to him with questions."

"Exactly."

"This is a lot… But it makes sense."

"I'm sorry." Raphael brushed his thumb over my knuckles, and my skin tingled under his touch.

"For what?"

"I should have told you before we mated."

I raised a brow. "I think we already covered the fact that I jumped you. I want to see your dragon."

"Sure, we can do that—"

"Now. Please. I just need to see him." I didn't know why, but intuition hadn't steered me wrong before. After all, it brought me here.

"There's more I need to tell you."

"After," I said.

He hesitated for a moment, and I thought perhaps he was going to deny me. Then he nodded. I bounced on my toes and clapped like a child being given a toy.

I tugged him toward the back door. "Is there enough room in the backyard? How big are you?"

He laughed. "Big enough. I'll fit in the backyard, though."

He followed me out the back and down the steps of the deck. I wrapped my arms around my middle and shivered. The cool morning air sent a chill through me. The morning dew made my feet wet as I walked through the grass.

I turned to face him. A smile played at his lips and his green eyes sparkled.

"Are you ready?" he asked.

I nodded. My breath hitched and my body thrummed with excitement. An hour ago, I didn't know shifters existed, and now I was going to watch my lover become a dragon.

Raphael stood still, his arms lifted and his eyes closed. Then the air thickened around us and energy crackled. It was like the air around him shifted and a green hue filled the space. His muscles rippled and expanded, bones changing shape. His skin turning from the golden hue to an emerald green.

In mere seconds, his dragon was in front of me. He towered over me by what felt like ten feet. His wings flexed and expanded, shadowing me.

"Holy shit. You're breathtaking." I stepped closer, lifting my hand.

A low rumble sounded from his belly, shaking the ground. He lowered his head. His snout was long, his eyes a silver hue that held intelligence. Down his long neck were ridges that stretched along his spine and down to the tip of his tail. A tail that was curving toward me, encircling me.

I held out a hand, and his snout touched my palm. His scales were warm under my touch and smooth. I traced the intricate pattern with my fingertips.

Mate.

I didn't know if that word came from me or from him, but either way, I knew it to be true.

"Mate? Are we mates, Raphael?"

Chapter 11

RAPHAEL

"I think we should go out to lunch," Luca said. "Or breakfast. Whatever time of day it is, we should have that meal."

We had come in from showing Luca my dragon. He reacted way better than I anticipated. I still felt awful for not having told him what I was before last night, but he understood.

"I feel like I can look at the town with new eyes now. Also, I have a ton of questions."

I chuckled. "Yeah, I suppose you will. If you want to go out, we can go out."

"While we're out, why don't we get your things from the fire station? There's no reason for you to stay there when I have a perfectly good house. You can stay here with me."

I raised a brow. "Moving in together? So soon?"

"We are mates, aren't we?"

My dragon rumbled with pleasure. Luca felt it when I was in my scales. The word had echoed between us like a rope tying us together. An unbreakable bond.

"We are indeed," I said. "I'll only move in if you're sure, Luca. I don't want to rush things."

"That ship sailed last night, love."

We had so much more to talk about, but I sensed my mate still processing it all. I could practically see the gears working in his mind as he took it all in.

"Not having you near me would distress me more than trying to follow some silly idea of what the proper timeline is for a relationship. The house will feel empty without you. You said yourself you were drawn to it."

"All right." I wrapped my arms around his middle and pulled him to me. "Lunch first. Then the fire station."

"Perfect."

"Let's walk."

He grinned. "Of course."

We walked together, hand in hand, down the side street to Main.

"A lion shifter lives there." I pointed at the house four doors down from Luca's

"Mrs. Schaffer is a lion?"

"Yep."

"Huh. I would have assumed she was a bear. Is it offensive to ask people what their species is? I don't want to offend anyone."

"No. Now that you know about them, they won't be insulted."

"How did they keep this from me for so long? Am I the only one in town who didn't know?"

I nodded. "Normally, they would have driven outsiders out of town since they want to keep themselves private and their secret safe, but everybody liked you. They wanted to keep you."

The smile that spread across my mate's face made me happy.

"Aw, that's so nice. Did Tyler tell you that?"

"He did. I think everyone will be relieved that you know now. They were all hoping you'd find your mate among them. You did walk in on several situations that they were sure would give them away."

"I did notice that everybody goes quiet when I enter a room."

I chuckled. "Yep, that would be why."

We were on Main Street now. There weren't many people out and about, but those that were waved at us. I held the door open to the café, and Luca walked inside. Michelle squealed when she saw him, rushing to his side and wrapping her arms around him.

"Oh, finally! I'm so happy for you!"

Luca raised a brow, looking from me to her and back again.

"Your scent has changed," she said. "He explained things, right? Dragon, you better have explained things to him before you did the deed." She glared at me, and even though I towered over her by a foot, I felt about six inches tall.

"They can tell that we..." Luca cleared my throat. "There are no secrets here, huh?"

"Indeed, there are not," Michelle added. "Oh, Luca, we're so happy for you. We had hoped that you would find someone here. That's why we kept introducing you to everyone. But when no one clicked, we decided that we would keep you and just be careful. And look, it all worked out!"

I grinned and squeezed Luca's hand. "It did all work out." Even if I hadn't quite explained all the things to him. We had time.

"Are you guys coming in for lunch?" Michelle asked.

"Yes, please," Luca said. "We're starved."

She laughed. "I just bet you are."

Throughout our meal, we couldn't seem to go a minute without someone stopping by and saying hello. News had traveled fast. Each person offered their well-wishes and congratulations. The more people that visited, the wider Luca's smile became.

"I didn't know I was so popular," he said.

"People love you. I can see why."

The scarlet on his cheeks darkened.

Tyler came in and sat down at our table briefly. "Welcome to the pack, Luca. Theo is going to be ecstatic. He's been petitioning me for weeks to be able to tell you about us. I was just about to break down and break all our rules. Now I don't have to."

"Only mates can know, huh?" Luca asked.

Tyler nodded. "Or under special circumstances, family members of mates. But yes, we don't just tell any human. Even if they are as cute as you." Tyler winked at him, and my dragon roared to the surface.

Luca's eyes widened. "Down, boy. He was just teasing."

I stilled. "You could feel that?"

Luca nodded. "Yeah. Little jealous, were you?"

It was my turn to blush.

Luca slid closer to me, and I wrapped my arm around his shoulder. He turned back to Tyler. "Well, your secret is safe with me. Thank you for always welcoming me, even though it seems I was quite the liability to have around."

Tyler smiled. "It was our pleasure. And see? It all worked out." He slid out of the booth and clapped Luca on the back. "Now the two of you are stuck here. You're never leaving your pack now."

"Thank you," I said.

"This feels crazy," Luca murmured after Tyler left. "A person shouldn't be this happy this soon, right?"

"It's okay," I reassured him, squeezing his hand again. "It's more than okay."

"I think I'm ready to hear more about what this mate thing means," he said.

"It means exactly what you would expect. You are my mate. My partner. The person who is perfect for me in all ways. The same way that I am perfect for you. Now that my dragon knows you and your scent, I will never care for another. I will never look at another the way that I look at you. You are it for me."

"Wow. That's intense."

"It is. All shifters, not just dragons, search for their mates. Well, most of them anyway. I suppose some don't wish to be tied down."

"But you do?"

"I do. I've always wanted to find my mate, and I'm so very glad I found you."

Luca sighed and leaned into me. The warmth of his body radiated against my skin. "I am too, dragon. I didn't even know I was searching for you, but I feel complete now that I have you. Which is why I'm never letting you go. You're moving in. Today."

"You won't hear an argument from me," I said.

Chapter 12

LUCA

Raphael and I made our way across the street to the large park where everyone in town had gathered. The park was on the opposite side of town than the fire station, but since it was such a small town, it was still only a short walk from our house. I carried a container of pasta salad I had put together for the occasion. Apparently, pack gatherings were potluck style, and we needed to bring a dish. Raphael carried our cooler full of drinks—a six-pack of beer for him and sparkling water for me.

"Luca, there you are!"

Theo raced toward me and wrapped his arms around me. "You smell so different," he said. His eyes lit up, and the happiness radiated off him. He had been texting me almost non-stop since Raphael and I mated, asking details that I was not going to share over text. The heathen even had the audacity to ask for pics. I was only slightly tempted to send them.

I laughed when he stuck his nose closer to my neck and inhaled. I was still getting used to the idea that everyone smelled me.

"Theo, this is Raphael, my mate," I said. The word still sounded a bit odd, but it made my dragon preen when I said it. I had tested out both the words "boyfriend" and "mate." Mate seemed to illicit a thrill of desire through Raphael's dragon, enough that I felt it through our bond.

Theo narrowed his eyes at Raphael and pointed a finger at him. "I know it goes against our nature to ever do anything to harm our mates, but I swear on all the full moons that if you ever do anything that even upsets my friend even a little bit, I'll turn you into mincemeat."

Raphael's eyes widened, and then he broke out into a grin. He put his arm around my shoulder and pulled me closer to him. With my dragon as my personal heat source, I'd never need another winter coat. "I would never dream of harming Luca in any way, and I am so very glad he has a friend like you."

"Well, then." Theo straightened, mischief returning to his eyes. "I suppose you'll do. But don't you dare get in the way of our omega night, okay? We'll watch movies until dawn and kick you out of your own house. No complaints."

"You'll get none from me. I suppose that's where my three-on, three-off shifts will come in handy."

"Oh, perfect! You could not have picked a better mate," Theo said, linking his arm into mine. Raphael's arms slid off my shoulder as Theo pulled me away.

I smiled at Rafael when he winked at me. I hadn't expected my friend to do that, but then again, I wasn't surprised.

"So how have I never noticed that there is a big gathering like this on every new moon?" I asked.

Tyler had filled us in when he had stopped by and extended the invitation for Raphael and me to attend the pack gathering. On the full moon, the pack shifted and ran together, but they used the new moon as an excuse to get together for a shared meal and just enjoy their time together.

"Oh, we've been having them out in the woods. Old man Fisher has a cabin out there. He wasn't too thrilled about us invading, but when we explained that we were trying to keep it from you, he was fine with it. You won him over when you checked on him after that nasty infection he got a few months ago."

I recalled the incident. We had been sent out by Tyler to check on Mr. Fisher who preferred to live deeper in the woods, secluded from everyone. He was reluctant to get any treatment for a cut on his hand that got infected after a fishing incident.

"We've also had to make the events during your shifts, so that way you wouldn't notice when we weren't all around."

"Oh. Well, now I feel a little bad that you all had to hide from me."

"I told Tyler many times that you needed to be looped in," Theo huffed. He gripped my arm tightly like he was afraid I might run away.

"That man never listens to me. I didn't want to lose my bestest friend, and we couldn't keep hiding forever."

"And I told you numerous times, we can't tell humans about us just because you like them," Tyler said as he came up to Theo's side and ruffled his hair.

Theo shot him a glare. "Clearly my instincts were correct and it would have been perfectly fine to tell Luca."

Other members of the fire department came over and shook Raphael's hand, giving me a nod and welcoming me to the pack.

"You guys really hid all of this just so I wouldn't find out?" I asked. "Gosh, it seems like it would have been easier just to run me out of town."

"Absolutely not," Theo said. The horror on his face was comical. "Tyler and I had numerous conversations about that as well. That jerk was on the side of running you out of town."

"Before I met him, Theo!" Tyler turned his sharp gaze on Theo and pinned him with a stare that would have most cowering. Theo didn't flinch. "And it's Alpha to you, cub." Tyler turned back to me. "We're happy to have you here, Luca. And we're so very glad you and Raphael have found each other."

"I agree," Bernice chimed in.

All around me, everyone nodded. Tyler, who I now knew was the pack leader, Levi who had helped train me when I first started as an EMT, Michelle who made my coffee each morning, and a whole lot of other people who I'd met either in town or while on various paramedic runs.

"We like you, Luca. We wanted you to stay," Michelle said. "We talked about it as a group and not a single person wanted to run you out once they met you. And trust me, we've given the cold shoulder to plenty of humans to get them to leave town."

Thank goodness I had my mate here to hold me up, because I was about to collapse into a fit of tears—happy tears, of course.

"Remember when you first moved here, you thought it was so weird that we all referred to the town as territory?" Tyler laughed. "Theo told me about that."

"Well, it is weird," I said.

Raphael's arms encircled my waist, his fingertips working their way underneath the hem of my shirt until our skin touched. I leaned into the comfort of his embrace, feeling at home not just in his arms, but also by all these wonderful people.

Theo rolled his eyes. "All mates are ridiculous. You all just can't keep your hands off each other. Keep it PG, will you? This is a family event."

"No promises," Raphel said.

"Well, this is the whole event," Tyler said. "Different events have different activities, but this is mostly just eat and enjoy yourself. I won't be giving any particular speeches or anything here. When it comes time to officially welcome you both into the pack, we'll schedule that right before a pack run. I have a team of people who like to make it all official, fill out the paperwork, and all that. This event is just for fun."

"Thank you," Raphael said, shaking Tyler's hand again. "Thank you for including us."

"Absolutely, man. And like Theo said, you do anything to hurt our Luca, you'll answer to us."

I turned to Raphael as we sat down at a picnic table. Both of us had filled our plates—Raphael's high enough to necessitate needing two, but he still only had one. The paper strained under the weight of the food.

He winked when he caught me looking. "Shifter trait. We eat a lot."

"I'll say."

We were quiet for a moment. I looked around at everyone. There were so many people that I knew, all of them enjoying the gathering.

"I can't believe they all went to such lengths to keep this all a secret from me. I feel terrible that they all had to hide themselves like that."

"They love you. You shouldn't be surprised at how much everyone likes you, Luca. You're amazing."

"You're biased," I said.

He chuckled. "Perhaps, but that doesn't change the fact."

Chapter 13

RAPHAEL

"Tomorrow, we'll be back to our regular schedules," I said to Luca once we settled onto the couch in our living room. Luca snuggled close to my side, resting his head on my chest, his arm draped over my middle. I hugged my arm around his shoulder.

There was not a moment in the past week in which the two of us didn't spend touching one another. The instinct to keep my mate close and protected at all times was strong, and I didn't try to fight it. I liked him close by where I could smell the freshness of his scent.

"When does your shift start?" he asked.

"Seven, same as yours, except I have three days on."

"The house will be lonely without you," he said. His lips turned down in a pout, then he blinked it away as if he was going to be strong for me.

"I know it," I agreed. "Luckily, you aren't far away."

"What's the policy on mates staying at the station?" Luca hugged me tighter, like he wanted to crawl into my skin.

I laughed. "Unfortunately, you can visit but not stay the night." Not that I had double-checked the policy or anything.

"Surely, Tyler will let us break the rules."

I laughed heartily at that. "If only. Technically as a new hire I'm still on probation, so I probably shouldn't break the rules." I doubted Tyler would fire me, but I didn't want to find out.

"We will be fine, mate. I know how important your work is."

My dragon rumbled happily at that.

"He likes when I call you mate."

"You can feel him?"

"I can—a lot. Is that normal?" Luca toyed with the hem of my shirt as if he was considering taking it off me.

"It is," I said. "At least, I think it is. Obviously, you're the only mate that I have."

"I better be," he said, and he poked my middle.

"I want you to meet my brothers."

"I'd love that," Luca said. "Have you told them about me?"

I nodded. "I sent them messages. They had a lot of questions. Both of them are on their own journeys right now. Once things settle, we will all have to get together." We had a lot to talk about. Based on the details they'd shared, they had each been on their own exciting adventures as well.

"Do you think that we'll stay here or move to be closer to them?"

"I don't know," I said. "I kind of assumed we would stay here. I like it here, in this house. It feels like home."

"Me too," Luca said. "And even though it's only been a few days, I like the idea of starting a family with you, putting down our roots here. The pack loves us, and our children would be surrounded by other shifter children."

I kissed the top of his head, then rested my cheek against his hair. "I love that idea, too."

"You and your brothers were one clutch," Luca said. "Three eggs?"

"Yes."

"Is that a typical number? Or should we be worried that we might have more than three dragonets?"

"Maybe," I said.

"Three just sounds like a lot."

"It is, although multiple births are pretty typical for dragons and even wolves."

"I'll be honest, that's kind of terrifying." Luca's hand was fully under my shirt now, trailing up my torso. I wondered if he even realized he was doing it. Our instincts were to be as close to each other as possible.

"Fate would not give us more than what we can handle. I promise."

"Oh, don't get me wrong, multiple children with you would be amazing. I have always wanted a big family. But three at once—"

"I know. It will be challenging." Terrifying. Exciting. I couldn't think of a better person to take on that challenge with.

"How soon will we know?"

I shrugged. "I'm not sure. We can ask Quinn. He is the pack doctor."

"Wait. I thought he was the vet."

"He runs the vet clinic also. He went to vet school, but there are many cases where animal science helps diagnose issues in shifters better than human medicine, so that's pretty typical. Tyler also mentioned there is a group of doulas in town that can also help."

"I suppose that makes sense, especially if one is injured in their shifter form. Don't you shifters heal very fast? I mean, your burns disappeared within a day."

"We do, but there are some things that even we can't come back from."

Luca shuddered. "That's not something I want to hear, not when I know how dangerous your job is."

"I am always careful, mate. Always." I kissed his head, letting my lips linger over his skin. His body thrummed with pleasure. "Now that we are mated, you also have my healing abilities. You cannot shift, of course, but there are benefits to being mated to a dragon."

Luca giggled but said nothing.

"What?" I asked.

"I was just thinking that your cock was the benefit... but I'll take rapid healing as well."

I chuckled and tickled his side until he squealed.

"So, wolves enjoy the full moon, based on what I learned at the event today."

"They do."

"The bear shifters mentioned that they have a hibernation where they just kind of lie low for a few weeks."

"They do."

"So what about dragons?"

"What about them?" I asked.

"Well, do you have a hoard?"

I chuckled. "Perhaps. Is that something you would like to see?"

"Maybe," he said, and he poked me in my stomach again. "Is it something I'm allowed to see?"

"Absolutely. Wait right here."

I had been waiting for just the right time to share my small hoard with my mate. Like many dragons, I was attracted to shiny things. Not all dragons hoarded items, though. The instinct was unique to each dragon.

I went to the spare room where I had placed my footlocker that held many of my items. I opened it, moved some of the things aside, and finally found my treasure chest. It was small but heavy, thanks to the contents inside. I picked it up. It was small in size, but it held all the treasures I had acquired over time—some of which I had inherited from my parents, others I had found. The chest itself had been made especially for me a few years ago.

I carried it into the living room and set it down.

Luca's eyes widened when he took it in. The sunlight shining through the window gleamed off the emerald jewels that lined the top of it. There were also jade and peridot gems inlaid on the slats and trim.

"Holy shit, Raphael. That's a treasure chest. Like a pirate's treasure chest!"

"Well, it didn't belong to any pirates. Ever. I had it made for me."

"No kidding? It looks old."

"Some of the pieces have been reclaimed. The jewels on it were gifted to me—the top emerald from my parents, the two rubies from my brothers, Brock and Nolan."

"But what's inside?"

"That's the amazing part."

I called forth my dragon. He alone could unlock it. The lockplate was specially crafted so that when it was at regular temperature the chest was locked, but if it was heated to a certain degree it would unlatch. Once it was unlatched, I opened it up.

Luca gasped when he looked inside. There was an assortment of gold coins, jewels, and various gemstones.

"Raphael, this is beautiful."

"Thank you," I said. "It's yours. The hoard is meant to be for a mate—to impress them. Everything I have gathered and put away in here has been for you."

"I love it," he said. "But more than that, I love you. I know it's silly by human standards. We shouldn't feel this way already. But you're mine."

"I love you too, mate. I am yours. Always."

Chapter 14

LUCA

At least right now, my schedule aligned nicely with Raphael's. I worked three days of twelve-hour shifts while he worked three days of twenty-four-hour shifts, then we each had three days off. Although it was only day two, I missed him.

He was across the street from me all day, unless he or I were out on a call. Sometimes, I saw him in the window and waved. Sometimes, around mealtimes, if there wasn't an emergency going on, I would sneak across the street and see him. For the most part, I tried to get through my days without being too attached to my mate, which seemed silly. It shouldn't be this hard to be separated from a man I just met. Maybe that was too much of a human mindset. As far as I could tell, it was perfectly normal for mates to be incredibly attached to one another.

In fact, now that I knew about shifters and mates, I could see it in the world around me—like how Mrs. Benson and her mate, Gerald, ran the hardware store together, and how Olivia and Sue were always seen together, never apart. The two of them ran the bar in town, and it was quite famous for its 80's nights. I had never gone, though Theo had begged me to a few times.

So it was perfectly normal for me to want to be near my mate all the time. Except the two of us had jobs to do. Both of us were relatively new to town, and I wasn't going to jeopardize our positions because I was feeling clingy.

Unfortunately, this particular shift was going agonizingly slow. I missed my mate, and my stomach was rolling. I had barely been able to keep down a cup of coffee this morning. Sleep had been restless.

For years, I had lived without sleeping next to a person. Suddenly, Raphael was in my bed for just a couple of days, and now I couldn't sleep without him. I needed a dragon-sized pillow to cuddle when he wasn't there. Thankfully, online shopping had proven quite fruitful in that endeavor, and I had two different ones arriving this week. They weren't actually dragon shaped, though when I'd found a fluffy green one, I'd been tempted.

My phone pinged with a text, and I opened it up. It was Theo.

Theo: Any special requests? I'm stopping by for a visit.

As far as I could tell, Theo worked whatever hours he wanted to, and apparently, today was one of the *not-want-to* days. On those days, he tended to visit—which I loved. He was the bestest best friend I could've ever asked for. It must have been agonizing for him not to be able to share his full self with me. But now he could.

Me: Ginger ale?

He replied with a question mark.

I sent back: Yes.

Twenty minutes later, Theo walked in the door. He held a large thermos and a brown paper sack. The smell that wafted off of the thermos was sweet, and my mouth watered.

"That is not ginger ale," I said.

"It's something better." He hesitated. "Now, this is not an appropriate question, so slap me if you'd rather I not ask… but—"

"Yes, I do suspect I'm pregnant."

He squealed and jumped on his toes, running in place while he clapped happily. "Oh, I'm so happy! Listen, ginger ale is not going to do jack shit for a shifter pregnancy. Especially a dragon pregnancy or whatever it's called when you are carrying eggs."

I raised a brow.

"So I brought you some of the stuff my mom swears by. You know she runs that little apothecary shop, right?"

"The place that sells the special teas?"

"Exactly. Everyone comes to her when they're expecting because she's got the best stuff for morning sickness. She even has good stuff if your blood pressure goes wonky later on."

"Fingers crossed that won't happen."

"Oh, I wouldn't worry about that for you, sweetheart. You're carrying *dragons*. You'll be laying eggs, not little cubs or pups, right?"

That was terrifying to think about.

Any time I had thought about having children before, it was always a baby, a nine-month pregnancy. But now, I was having *eggs*. And how long was that gestation, exactly? I had no fucking clue.

"Here." He set the thermos down, then grabbed a coffee mug from the little kitchenette. "I told her you like sweet things and cinnamon, so this should taste almost like a cinnamon roll."

It sure smelled like one.

"Now, you can only have a cup in the morning. You don't want to overdo it, or it won't work as well. It's meant to ease the suffering, not take it completely away—which sucks, but it's better than nothing."

"I'll take it," I said. "I can't imagine doing a few months of this."

"Oh, dragon pregnancies are way shorter. You're going to lay eggs in a couple of weeks."

"How do you know all this?"

He shrugged. "My dad's a historian. I started asking some questions right after you and Raphael mated. I had to pass the time somehow since my best friend was occupied."

"Maybe I should ask him some questions."

"It wouldn't be a bad idea. Or talk to your mate. Perhaps his family can clue you in."

"I will," I said. "We've just been busy."

Theo smirked. "Busy? I know what it means for mates to be busy. Ya'll just couldn't keep it in your pants."

I grinned, because he was not wrong. I sipped the tea slowly. He was right, the flavors were just perfect, and it was like drinking a liquid cinnamon roll. The temperature was also just right, making it easy to drink.

Already, the tea was starting to help. My stomach calmed, and the thought of eating a little something didn't send me hurtling toward the bathroom.

"Oh, thank you," I said, leaning back in my chair. "This stuff is amazing. I still don't know for sure if I'm pregnant."

"Don't you have, like, pregnancy tests here?"

"Um... maybe? We have those little strip thingies, I think. We were sent them by accident with our supplies last month, and I didn't know what to do with them."

"Well, let's grab one! Let's do it!"

"Shouldn't I do this with my mate?"

"Wouldn't it be way cooler to do it right now with your best friend, and then you can find a super special way to show him later? Besides, don't you want to know as soon as possible?" Theo's eyes danced with excitement, and he was bouncing again.

I groaned, because he was not wrong. I did want to know right now. And I would find a way to tell Raphael later.

"Fine, fine."

I gulped down the rest of the tea, my stomach finally settling. Already, it was like my stomach evened out, and my skin felt better, no longer clammy and tight.

"Oh, wow. Your mom is a miracle worker."

"She really is," he said. "You don't know the half of it. She's also a certified doula. Obviously, she's used to bear pregnancies, but I am sure she would love to help you with yours."

Theo disappeared into the supply closet.

I suppose I should be concerned about a non-employee going through our things, but, well, he did work for the town, so I guess that wasn't the same as a random person snooping.

"Perfect! We've got one."

Theo began to follow me toward the bathroom.

I turned to him. "I think I can manage this part alone."

He smiled so big.

"What?" I asked.

"I'm just so happy for you and Raphael. Selfishly, I'm also happy for me. I spent weeks crafting an argument for Tyler about why you should know about us. He was just about to give in. I'm sure of it."

"I'm really glad I have you too, Theo. Soon to be Uncle Theo."

He squealed and hugged me tight. "Exactly. Uncle Theo! Now go in there. Get this done."

Minutes later, two lines stared back at me.

Positive.

Raphael and I were going to have little dragonets.

Chapter 15

RAPHAEL

Hopefully, being away from my mate while I was on shift would get easier with time. More than once, I was tempted to have him sneak into the station and stay the night with me. I just wanted to hold him in my arms. We wouldn't even be inappropriate at all. Promise.

As soon as my shift was over, I picked up my things and got ready to leave. If anyone asked me to work a double, I would lose my mind. Each passing moment I prayed the alarm wouldn't go off and I'd be stuck on a call. I couldn't bear to be away from Luca any longer.

Tyler came over, smiling like a wolf who had captured a bunny.

"What?" I asked.

"Nothing," he said. "I just lost a bet because of you."

"What bet?"

"Levi was sure that you would sneak your mate into the dorm at some point this weekend or sneak over there for some hanky-panky. But no, you two had to play it cool and follow the rules. I sided with Levi, AJ bet you'd be able to make it three days."

I rolled my eyes. "Don't think I wasn't tempted."

"But you didn't do it," Tyler said.

"No. Don't remind me that it's been three days since I've had my mate in my arms. I'm barely containing my dragon as it is."

Tyler grinned. "Listen, he can come around the station as much as he wants. The two of you don't have to worry so much about what's proper and what's normal. Luca especially needs to know that everything might feel fast because he's human, but you're mates. This is in your biology. Don't fight the instincts, okay? And if you need more time off, we can make that happen."

"Thanks, Tyler. I appreciate it. It's very likely my mate is expecting, and we'll be negotiating some time off for when the eggs arrive and then when they hatch. So I might just save what little time off I have." Which was almost nothing, since I had just started this job.

Tyler grinned. "Congratulations! I'm always happy to have more members of the pack."

I held up a hand, stopping him before he could get too excited. "I don't even know for sure. It is rather soon. We've only been mated a week."

"Of course. Now get out of here. Get home to your mate."

I didn't have to be told twice. I slipped my bag over my shoulder and slid down the pole. Yes, we had a pole in the fire station.

There was soft music playing when I entered the house. The curtains were all drawn, and the place was dark, though it was just a little after seven in the evening.

"Luca?" I called, sensing that he was here.

"In here," he called back. His voice came from the back of the house, where the living room was.

I wasn't expecting what I found in the living room. Next to the large bay window, the couch had been pushed aside, and now there was an assortment of soft, pillow-like things all arranged in a nest-like form. My mate, wearing a pair of short shorts and a tank top, lay in the center. He was surrounded by colorful blankets of varying sizes. One was a plush fleece, the other a velvet material.

"I'm really glad you're here. I've been busy today," he said.

"I see that. Where did all this come from?"

"Theo and I went shopping. I grabbed everything that felt right."

He held his hand out, a small item resting in his palm. My heart rate increased. I stepped forward, my breath catching in my throat. Already, my dragon suspected what my human side was only now realizing.

I needed to see it for myself.

I grabbed the item in his hand. "I don't know what I'm looking at. Is this... is it a pregnancy test?"

Luca grinned and nodded. "It is. I'm sorry that I took one without you and that Theo was with me, but I had to know. This morning, I started feeling not so great. Thankfully, Theo's mom is a miracle worker, and he brought me tea she makes. Did you know she is a doula?"

"And all this?" I gestured to the nest.

Luca looked down at the nest he stood in, and his brow furrowed. "I don't know. Once I realized I was pregnant—and that I was going to have eggs, of all things—I thought they probably needed a place to go. Right? Someplace warm and cozy. I just... followed my instincts and got what I felt made sense."

"Indeed, they do need a nest." I grinned, my dragon roaring to the surface at the news of our clutch.

"Good. So I bought all of this. What do you think?"

"You did perfect, mate. I'm so proud of you."

I was about to tug him upward so I could hold him, but instead, he pulled me down. The softness of the perfect nest my mate had put together wrapped me in its embrace. Luca draped himself over me, pulling one of the thicker fleece blankets around us. The pillows were soft, but there were enough of them that I couldn't even feel the floor beneath it.

"Oh, wow," I said. "This really beats the beds at the station."

"I know, right? It might be better than the bed we have."

"Our eggs are going to be very cozy here. Whenever they're laid. You did so well, mate." I kissed him soundly, putting as much love as I could into the kiss. Luca melted against me.

"Do you know how long I'll carry them?"

I settled back into the pillows and Luca laid his head on my chest. "It varies from dragon to dragon, but definitely a month, probably closer to six weeks. You have some time."

"Oh, good, because I really want to carry them." He grabbed my hand and placed it over his flat tummy. "They're in there," he said. "I don't know how many. I'm hoping two, but they are there."

"They are," I said, kissing his cheek. "I'm so excited."

"Good. Since we have the next three days off, I did make an appointment with Dr. Quinn. He said that he doesn't have any experience with dragon pregnancies, but he's prepared to help in any way he can. And we can reach out to Theo's mom about being our doula."

"Fantastic," I said, wrapping Luca in my arms and pulling him close. I tugged the blankets that covered the pillows over us.

"This is a beautiful nest, mate. I'm so proud of you."

"Are you hungry at all? I lost track of time, I didn't even make you dinner or anything."

"Later," I said. "Right now, I just want to be right here. I had three very long days without you, and I can't spend another minute without you next to me."

Luca sighed, settling into my embrace. The warmth of him in my arms caused my eyes to droop. Sleep was just within my reach.

"The bed was empty without you. I could barely sleep without you next to me."

"Me too, love. Me too."

Chapter 16

LUCA

On the day of the next new moon, both Luca and I had the day off. We had a lazy morning, drinking our coffee near the nest. At some point, I shifted for a while and lay in the nest with Luca curled up at my side. He read a book, something about what to expect when expecting. Even though he wasn't carrying a human baby, he said some of the human texts were still helpful.

He held his book with one hand, and with the other, he lazily stroked my scales. I let out a rumble of contentment, and he laughed.

"We should get up, dragon. It's time to go to the gathering."

I let out a deep sigh, smoke furling from my nostrils.

"I know you want to be lazy all day, especially now that I have these sun lamps turned on."

Luca had insisted that the nest wasn't going to be warm enough since the window didn't get adequate sun in the evening, so he bought grow lamps. I had to admit, they were amazing. After a long shift at the fire station, I would change to my dragon form and lie near the nest. I barely fit in the room. We had to get rid of the couch—not that I was going to complain.

When my dragon form wasn't in here, the room looked rather sparse, but still, it was important for me to be close to my eggs once they hatched. My dragon would want to be there.

For now, Luca and I spent time in the nest making sure our scent was as present as possible so once the eggs were laid, they would sense us there even if we weren't with them.

"Come on, dragon, we've got to go."

Luca got up from where he sat. He stepped over my tail.

I shifted, shrinking down in size until I was just a mere human man, lying in my nest naked.

"As gorgeous as that view is, I'm not going to let you distract me," Luca said. He snapped his fingers. "C'mon. I don't want to be late."

I let out a sigh and finally got to my feet. Today we would be attending our second new moon gathering, and it seemed my mate was even more excited about this one. In the month that we'd been mated, it seemed that we were welcomed even deeper into the pack.

Within a few minutes, I was dressed and ready to go. We walked hand in hand toward the park. I carried the cooler in my other hand. Inside was some sort of salad my mate had put together.

He had a slight swell to his stomach now. The doctor had confirmed that we were carrying eggs—just two. There was still a chance that there were twin dragons inside one of the eggs, but we wouldn't know until they were laid. I thought two was a beautiful number.

The park was set up slightly differently than the last time we were there. The last time had just been a regular celebration. This time, it looked like a party. There were balloons in soft pastel colors and various decorations on all the tables. It wasn't until we got closer that I realized what it was.

The banner at the first table read:

Congratulations, Raphael and Luca!

Of course, Theo was there, right away at my mate's side.

"We're so glad you're here! Although, I was hoping you would be a little late. I'm still putting together a few last-minute things."

"Theo, what is this?" Luca asked.

"A baby shower. Duh."

Luca's eyes welled up with tears. He fanned his face. "Theo—"

"Oh, don't cry, because then I'll cry."

"Yes, please don't let Theo cry," Tyler said. "He will be reduced to a puddle of goo, and I'll have to do all the rest of the work." Theo slapped at his chest playfully. Tyler dodged it. Tyler shook my hand. "Congratulations again. Welcome to your party."

"Thank you," I said. "We—we didn't expect this." There was a buffet table like the last time and next to it was a table stacked high with gifts.

"Well, we had to do a bit of a rush job. Now that we know there are two of them, we don't know what day Luca will be laying the eggs, and, well, we wanted you guys to be prepared."

The whole town was here, as they always were.

Luca swiped at his eyes and held my hand. "Thank you, this... this means so much to us," he said.

After we ate, Theo insisted that Luca sit down near the table where gifts were piled two and three high. My heart warmed. I was so lucky to have found this place—to have found my mate here.

One by one, Luca unwrapped our gifts. I kept track of the cards, writing down who had brought what so we could send thank-you notes later.

"Oh, that one's from me," Theo said, pointing at a bright pink bag with dark red and black tissue paper. "That one's not safe for opening in public, and it's more for once the babies are here and you're feeling a bit more like yourself." He winked.

"Oh, goodness," Luca said. I didn't know what was in those bags, but I couldn't wait to find out. Luca blushed. "Thank you, Theo."

The guys from the fire station carried in two large boxes, hastily wrapped in what looked like trash bags and duct tape.

"You really should have let me handle that, Tyler," Theo said.

"Hush," Tyler said. "It's not about the wrap job. It's about the thought or whatever. Open it up."

I helped Theo pull apart the trash bag to reveal two brand-new, matching cribs.

"Wow," I said.

"Thanks, guys," Luca added.

"That comes with free assembly, too," Tyler said. "Levi drew the short straw. He'll be over tomorrow to help you put them together."

"Thanks," I said. "This really means a lot to us."

The warmth and camaraderie radiating from everyone in the park enveloped me. We had truly found our home here.

Luca finished unwrapping the gifts. We would need a truck to carry it all back to our home. Thankfully we had started on the nursery and it was ready to be filled. I had painted the room while Luca had picked out the few decorations, and now it was ready to be filled with furniture. We had been waiting until the eggs were laid.

Along with the gifts, we had amassed quite a selection of stuffed animals—ranging from dragons to unicorns to wolves and bears. Each present was a testament to the thoughtfulness of our friends. Our pack.

Susette, the wife of the man whose barn had burned, had painted a lovely picture of the landscape of the town, with one green dragon flying overhead, followed by two smaller dragons. It was beautiful. When I first opened it, I hadn't been able to find words to express my gratitude.

Luca faced the crowd. "Thank you. We're so overwhelmed by all your kindness. Thank you for taking me in and welcoming me into your lives. I... I just love it here. Our children are going to be so happy here with all of you."

Everyone applauded.

I held Luca's hand.

"Truly. Thank you all. I've worried about how my young dragons will fit in, but not anymore. I know that you'll accept them as they are, just as you've accepted Luca and me. We're very blessed to have found this place, and we can't wait to share our family with you all."

There was more applause and cheers as our friends and neighbors—our family—celebrated the start of our family.

Chapter 17

Raphael

Levi lined up his pool cue and struck the ball, sending not one but two of the striped balls into a pocket. He grinned at me, holding out his hand. I coughed up the few dollars that we had bet on this game. It was all in fun, and in a few more rounds, I'd probably win my money back. The loss still stung. Competitiveness was strong with this group, and I wasn't any different.

Apparently, the crew used to bet chores, but then they spent so much time playing pool to get rid of the chore responsibilities that the chores never got done. Now we bet with money.

"I'll tell you one nice thing about a fireman's hours and the random wake-up calls—it really prepares you for kids. There's no rhyme or reason to a kid's schedule. You're not going to get a lot of sleep for a while, then suddenly they'll start sleeping through the night, and you'll find yourself waking up, missing being able to snuggle them," Levi said.

I grinned. I couldn't wait for those days. Sleepless nights or not, I was ready. And he was right—our random hours at the fire station would do well to prepare both Luca and me for it. We frequently had to be awake at the drop of a hat, ready to do battle. That wasn't too far from what it would be like wrangling newborns in the middle of the night. Especially when there were two of them.

The alarm sounded, and our walkie-talkies started going off. It wasn't a fire—something else. Tyler sprinted up the stairwell, his face white, his eyes wide as he looked at me. That's when I knew something was wrong.

"We're being called out to an accident on the highway. It's a large pile-up, and they already have crews from surrounding towns out there."

I had seen and heard over the radio that my mate was out on a call. He had left not thirty minutes ago.

"They need additional paramedic crews? Luca just left for there."

We were already making our way down to the bays to get our gear and head out.

Levi grabbed his gear fist. I followed right behind him.

"We're taking the pickup truck," Tyler said.

"What?" That wasn't protocol. If we were responding as an assisting crew, we would take one of the smaller tankers.

"Just get in. I'll explain on the way. AJ, you stay here with the rest of the crew. Raphael, Levi, you're with me."

"What's going on?" I asked.

"Get in. I'll explain on the way."

My heart pounded, going a mile a minute. I searched through our bond, hoping to get something back from my mate. It was there. It was strong. But it wasn't as if we could communicate with one another through it.

My dragon rumbled beneath my skin as if he sensed something. All I could do was follow Tyler's lead.

I piled into the back while Levi drove and Tyler took the passenger seat.

Finally, once we pulled out onto the street, Tyler started talking. "There was an accident on the highway. We have multiple crews responding. Luca and Charlie made it there, but their ambulance was sideswiped by a—"

I sucked in a breath. "Sideswiped?" My mate had been hurt? It took everything in me not to shift immediately and fly out to where he was.

Tyler turned to look at me. His face held concern, but he was speaking to me as Alpha of the pack. "I don't know the details yet. Raphael, I'm going to need you to remain calm. When you get there, you have to keep hold of your dragon. Do you understand me? You cannot shift on a highway."

I nodded, my throat working. "I understand," I said. Obeying orders like I was one of his wolves wasn't typical for me, but desperate times and all that. I couldn't risk exposing us all as shifters in the middle of a crisis. Luca needed me to be strong.

Levi hit the gas, the engine roaring. Despite his speed, it felt like it took an agonizingly long time to get there. There were crews everywhere—a fire truck from a nearby town, two ambulances, multiple vehicles in various states of fender-bender. One was twisted on its side.

That's when I spotted it—Luca's ambulance. The side had been smashed in, the gurney lay on its side on the ground.

I was out of the truck before it even stopped.

An ambulance crew from somewhere was already there. Luca lay on the ground, already on a baseboard, his neck braced, but there was blood coming out of his ear and a cut on his head.

"Luca!" My voice broke at seeing my mate in such a state. My dragon roared in my ears, and a sob ripped from my throat.

"Sir, we're going to need you to step back!" One of the EMT's that was attending Luca gripped my arm and tugged me away from him.

"That's my mate," I said. "My husband!" The human in front of me had no doubt dealt with distraught spouses before, but he had no idea at the level of desperation that was coursing through my veins. I was seconds away from losing complete control and letting my dragon take over.

Tyler was there, commanding the scene. I didn't know what he said or did, but then it was just Levi, Tyler, and me attending Luca.

"Get a hold of Quinn—he's in labor." Tyler rattled off commands to Levi.

"What?" No. Sure, we were close to time—he was at five weeks—but it was still early.

"The eggs…" Luca moaned. Luca's eyes opened, glassy. Then he stared at me. "Raphael," he said. "The eggs. Are they—?" He couldn't move his head, but his eyes followed.

"Everything's going to be fine," I said, squeezing his hand. "Everything's going to be just fine."

"Where's Charlie?"

"They're fine," I said. I didn't know for sure, but at this point, I could only focus on my mate and getting him to safety. He needed medical attention that no one here was capable of giving him.

"We have to get him out of here and somewhere he can deliver these eggs—away from the prying eyes of humans," Tyler said.

Levi nodded. "He's already healing his injuries from the crash. The stress has likely caused the labor. It's progressing quickly."

"I'm in labor? The eggs are coming?" Luca asked, his voice panicked.

"Yes. Just focus on me." I kept my gaze locked on my mate's, letting everyone else around us take care of the logistics of getting us out of here. My priority was keeping him calm.

"Let's get him into the truck," Tyler said.

I held Luca's hand while Levi and Tyler worked on getting him onto the board and into the back of the truck. If we didn't at least make it look like we were taking care of an injured patient, people would question it. Of course, they would have even more questions if an omega laid eggs on the side of the highway.

As soon as we were in the truck, we removed the straps.

Luca did as he was told and kept a tight hold on my fingers. He squeezed when a contraction hit him.

"Raphael, dragon, I'm not going to make it. I'm going to have these eggs here."

"You'll make it. We're so close, love."

"Umm..." Levi's voice came from the front seat. "Unless I'm breaking a lot of laws, I'm not so sure we're going to get very far."

"Get us out of here," Tyler said. "We do not want these eggs born on the highway."

"Fuck!" Luca's heart rate increased, and he let out a long wail. "They're coming."

"On it." Levi hit the gas.

Chapter 18

LUCA

The crunching of metal and screeching of tires, the smell of burnt rubber—these were all things I would never forget. The blinding white pain that rocketed through my bones when the side of the vehicle hit me was indescribable. The pain had been instant and unbearable, almost to the point where I couldn't tell where it started.

I lost consciousness for a while, but even in that state, I had desperately tried to wrap a protective arm around my abdomen.

Protect my eggs. Protect my eggs.

That was the only thing I could think. If it wasn't for my newly acquired healing abilities thanks to my dragon mate, I would not be in good shape.

Now I was moving—though where, I didn't know. Raphael's calming embrace wrapped around me.

"Everything's going to be just fine, Luca. We're going to the doctor."

"Home," I said. "I want to have my eggs at home."

I was in labor now. The stress of the accident was too much for my body. My breaks and cuts had healed thanks to my dragon mate, but that didn't take away the stress my body had endured.

These eggs wanted out. Now.

The pressure in my abdomen was absolute torture. It was as if all the muscles in my body were conspiring together and squeezing all at once to get these eggs out.

"We are closer to your house than the clinic," Tyler said. "We can have Quinn meet us there."

"Yes," I said. "Do that."

The ride had been bumpy at first. I didn't know how Levi had gotten us out of there, I was just thankful that he had.

I was in the back seat of the fire truck. Oh goodness, I could not have my eggs in a fire truck. They needed to be in their nest, snuggled safe where they belonged. I didn't want to give birth in the back of a truck. I needed my nest. My perfect, beautiful nest.

Raphael and I had spent weeks perfecting the nest, and we were proud of it. The plan had been to have a quiet, comfortable birth there.

"Raphael, I'm scared. I'm so sorry."

"Hush. It's not your fault," he said. He brushed the hair from my forehead and kissed me. His lips lingered on my forehead, and he continued to murmur encouraging words to me while I rode out another contraction.

The truck came to a stop, and as much as I wanted to get out and go into my home, there was no time.

"They're coming," I said. "Holy shit, they're coming now." The pressure built to a point of no return. I could feel the eggs now. They had to be close.

Raphael's eyes widened. Scales erupted over his neck and down his chest.

"Calm, dragon. I promise everything's gonna be okay."

I had no idea if that was the case. Sure, I had inherited—or rather, gotten—his healing ability once we were mated, but there were some injuries you couldn't come back from. What damage had been done to my eggs in this mess? I couldn't bear it if something happened to them.

The back door opened, sunlight streaming in.

"Raphael, I've done this before. I can deliver your eggs," Tyler said.

Oh shit. This was happening. I was going to give birth in the back of a truck. A fire truck, no less.

Raphael nodded and squeezed my hand. "Luca, you can do this. okay? Just breathe with me."

Tyler used his strength to remove my pants. The rip was barely audible over my loud moaning. I could barely tell what was happening—all of my focus was on pushing the egg from my body. Tyler positioned me carefully, his hands gentle. We didn't have a ton of room to work with in the cramped backseat. Tyler stood outside the truck, while my feet were propped on the door frame. My head rested in my mate's lap.

"Okay, we're ready, Luca. Go ahead and push."

I bore down, squeezing my mate's hand as he whispered encouraging things in my ear, assuring me that our eggs were going to be perfect.

Then the first one slipped from my body.

I had always imagined having my child placed in my arms. I would hold their tiny body against mine and see their eyes. Instead, it was an emerald egg that was placed against me, shining brightly in the sun. Its scales matched that of my mate. I hiccupped a sob as I held it against me. It was smooth and warm.

"One more," Raphael said. "Just like this one. He's perfect."

Raphael took the egg from my arms so I could concentrate on delivering the second egg.

I nodded. "Okay. Okay. Next one."

The second egg was smaller than the first, or maybe it just felt that way since my body was used to it. Tyler carefully held it out to me, and I held it in my arms. This egg was also green. The smooth scales were warm against my skin.

Tyler stepped away. "I'll give you two a moment, and then we need to get you inside."

Raphael kissed my forehead while I held both eggs in my arms. They were no bigger than a gallon of milk. They might not have been squirming babies, but there was a bond forming between us. Inside these precious shells were my children.

"They're happy," I said. I didn't know how I could sense it, but I could. These were my babies.

"They are," Raphael agreed. "I can sense them—our son and our daughter."

One was just a little bit lighter than the other, but they were of similar size now that I could compare them. I sensed the same happiness from them that Raphael did.

"Are we sure they're all right?" I asked.

"They are. I can sense it. A little stressed, a little scared after that whole ordeal, but they'll be just fine and happy. Once you're ready, we'll get you and them into the nest. How do you feel?"

I laughed. "Like I was hit by a truck and then gave birth."

Raphael laughed too, but it soon turned to silent tears that streamed down his face.

"I was so scared, mate. So incredibly terrified."

"Me too. But I knew you would come."

He kissed my cheek and pressed his forehead to mine. "Let's never do that again, okay?"

"Deal."

Raphael got out and carefully swept me into his arms. I held our eggs while he carried me into the house. We went straight to the nest.

Raphael set me down so I could place the eggs in their spots. I had two quilts ready for them.

Raphael switched on the lamp and the two of us snuggled close to our clutch.

I marveled at the two tiny emerald eggs. They looked small now, they definitely hadn't felt small when they had been in me, nor when they had come out of me.

Their presences filled the room with a sense of rightness. Our family.

"Will their scales match the color of their eggs?" I asked.

"Yes. They will be green like me."

"Hmm. Hopefully their human forms look like me then," I said.

Raphael chuckled. "Indeed. They will be a wonderful mix of both of us."

"You two are going to be strong dragons. Daddy's sorry for the chaotic way you were brought into the world. But wasn't your other daddy amazing? He was our hero." I stroked each of the eggs as I spoke to them.

A hum came from inside them, so faint I could hardly feel it.

"Was that...?"

Raphael nodded. "They hear you."

I gasped. "Oh, my babies. I love you so."

Raphael's hand covered mine. "I love you, mate."

Chapter 19

RAPHAEL

It had been four days since my mate's accident. Four days since our two perfect eggs entered this world, and still, I could not bear to be away from him or them for very long. Tyler granted us time off, though I knew that Luca was determined to get back to work.

We planned to have an egg sitter at the house, talking and interacting with the eggs while we were away. Technically, they would be fine on their own, but they did best developmentally if there were people around—especially pack members. And it turned out there were plenty of people in the pack willing to hang out at our house and talk to the eggs.

In the days that followed the laying of the eggs, we had many visitors dropping off casseroles, bouquets of flowers, and little trinkets for the nest, including a few very nice handmade quilts and pillows.

"Is it weird that we can stay in here all day like this?" Luca asked.

He sat in the nest, his body curved around both eggs as he lazily stroked their shells. He wore a soft robe, open at the front so that he could have skin-to-shell contact with the eggs. Meanwhile, I lay in my dragon form, my head resting on the edge of the nest, my tail curved around the entire thing, my beautiful heat lamp on and warming my body.

I rumbled in response.

Luca laughed. "I'm going to take that as a no, it's not weird. It's perfectly normal, right?"

He laid his cheek against one of the eggs. "I miss carrying them," he said. "I thought I'd have a longer time carrying them. And their birth was so chaotic. I miss it."

I chuffed out a response. It wasn't the first time he had mentioned missing carrying them. His birth experience hadn't been the one that we had planned, but it was over now, and we couldn't do anything about it. We still grieved the loss of the experience.

I shifted back to my human form, then pulled a quilt over my body. "I know it is disappointing that things didn't work out the way you planned."

We both had to process the complicated emotions that came with our birth plan being totally upended by an accident.

He sighed, his cheek rubbing against one shell while he stroked the other. "I am grateful it all worked out. It's hard to complain when they are unharmed. We were lucky."

"We were. We can acknowledge our luck and also grief for the experience we missed."

"This is true."

"We can always have more." I grinned.

He shot me a glare. "Let's get through these two first, please."

I crawled into the nest with him and wrapped my arms around him and the eggs. I kissed his shoulder.

"Are you sure that you're ready to return to work tomorrow?"

He sighed. "Yes. For the last time, yes, I can work. You can work, and Theo's mom plans on coming over to spend time with the eggs. Theo will be here as well throughout the day."

"Great," I scoffed. "He'll teach them swear words."

"Oh, he most certainly will. He is going to be a terrible influence on them, but he is going to love them to bits. I know it."

"I know he will too, mate."

I held him close, rubbing my hand up and down his arm.

"You don't need to worry about me while I'm working," he said. "It was a freak accident. It's not going to happen again."

"You can't guarantee that," I said.

"No, I suppose I can't. But that is what makes life so precious, isn't it? The fact that it can be taken away from us at any time."

I gripped him more tightly at the very thought that I could lose him. "I just worry."

"I know. And I love you for it."

"I love you too."

I kissed him slowly, letting my body do the talking that didn't always come so easily. Luca was everything to me. The very center of my world and my entire reason for waking up each day. I would be lost without him.

Luca's hands threaded into my hair. "I'm not just ready to return to work, mate. I'm ready for other things as well."

I raised a brow. "Oh yeah?"

"Yes. But… not here. C'mon."

He tugged me upward, and I followed. I would always follow.

I let the quilt fall from my shoulders, dropping onto the hardwood floor. Luca's robe followed soon after. That's when I realized my mate had been totally nude under there.

My dragon let out a growl, surging to the surface at the sight of our mate's bare skin lit up by the soft morning light. Luca turned, his mischievous gaze sending shivers down my spine.

"See something you like?" he teased.

Once we were in the bedroom, I pulled him to my chest. His warm skin soft against mine. "What if we didn't return to work? What if we just stayed here? Just us and our eggs. Forever."

"If only, love." His laughter echoed in my ears. "Pretty sure someone would come looking for us eventually."

Hunger surged through me. Not for food, but for my mate. We had only held each other since the accident, and I desperately needed to claim what was mine. My body missed his in a way that was primal and unbound.

Luca backed away from me and laid himself on the bed, his hard cock jutting up from his body. Pre-cum beaded on the tip.

Every inch of my body thrummed with desire, and I prowled toward my mate. The energy in the room thickened as my gaze locked on Luca.

There were so many choices. I could torture my mate in so many different ways. Fuck him, blow him, jack him off, edge him to the point of oblivion before I finally relented and let him come.

In the end, I needed the taste of him on my lips.

I gripped him by his calves and pulled him toward the edge of the bed, then lowered to my knees.

His sweet cock pressed against my lips. His hips jerked as he writhed beneath me. I opened my mouth and enveloped his cock. Luca's hands went to my hair, holding my face while his hips did the work. I let him fuck my mouth, his cock filling me, pressing against my throat until my eyes watered.

I savored the taste of him. Each thrust of his hips pushed a growl from deep within my throat.

"Raphael," he gasped. "Oh fuck, that feels so good."

He writhed and moaned, sounds erupting from his throat like sweet music to my ears. My own cock lengthened, threatening to come hands-free against the edge of the bed.

My mate's moans grew louder, his thrusts more erratic as I chased his orgasm. I nearly had it. I closed my mouth around him and sucked, my cheeks hollowing out. My tongue flicked against the underside of his cockhead.

"Raphael! Oh fuck!" he cried out. He surged forward, his hips coming off the bed as he spilled down my throat.

I savored every drop. My dragon roared in satisfaction.

"Hmm. I could live on that."

Luca's chuckle came out breathless. His fingers lazily threading through my hair. "I won't complain."

Epilogue

LUCA

Today was the day. I was sure of it.

My paternity leave officially started yesterday. I would have six weeks off and then another six weeks where I would return only part-time. We had childcare lined up—it turned out that there were plenty of pack members willing to hang out with our dragonets while Raphael and I worked.

But first, I needed them to get here. And before that, I needed my mate to arrive.

I paced next to the nest, keeping one eye on the nest while I walked the length of the room. I had already texted him and called. As a last resort, I had reached out to Tyler. Still nothing.

A small fracture split the center of one of the eggs. Occasionally, both eggs would move as if the two dragonets were talking to one another, ready to explore—perhaps scheming together in a way that only siblings could.

I was about to climb into the nest with them when the sound of a siren reached my ears. It seemed awfully close.

I went to the front window just as the fire truck was turning down our road, sirens blaring, lights flashing. Then it stopped on the road.

I smiled as my mate leapt out and ran up the front walk. He wore his turnout gear. The straps of his suspenders flapping at his sides.

He burst through the front door. "I didn't miss anything, did I?" He was already shucking off his turnout jacket that held a scent of smoke and ash. His face was darkened with soot.

"Were you on a call?" I asked.

"Just a small one. We're done. Mostly. Tyler will have to do the paperwork."

I shook my head. I supposed I shouldn't be surprised that Tyler arrived to the hatching in the back of a firetruck. After all, the eggs had been laid in one. "You haven't missed anything. They've just started pressing against the shells."

Together, he and I went to the nest. It was the place where we spent a majority of our time.

In the few seconds that I had stepped away, our daughter had someone how managed to roll her egg over and she now had a crack that matched her brother's.

It was a race.

"They're coming! I think it's happening!" I could barely contain my excitement. We were about to meet our babies! I had longed for this day. We had spent countless hours in the nest in the past six weeks, watching as the eggs shook and occasionally moved enough to roll. The gentle hum of their happiness was a constant reminder that inside were our children. Mine and Raphael's.

Raphael knelt beside me, his gaze locked on the eggs.

Our daughter's egg had a small piece of shell totally broken off, and we could peek inside.

"There you go, little one. Just a little more," I encouraged.

Another crack echoed in the quiet room, this time from our son's egg. Both eggs began to rock gently. They really were competing for who could come out the fastest.

Raphael's and my gaze ping-ponged between watching one egg, then the other. One of them was bound to burst out soon.

"They are so eager!" I said.

"C'mon, babies, come see your dads." Raphael inched closer to them, but we didn't touch the eggs. They would be able to do this on their own.

With a sudden burst of energy, both eggs shattered. The shells crumbled to the bottom of the nest, and two tiny dragonets emerged. Their scales glimmered with shades of mint green. Their little tails unwound from where they were nestled close to their bodies inside the egg.

They blinked their green eyes up at us, and then they began to chirp excitedly.

"Beautiful," Raphael breathed.

"They are," I said. I held out my hands, and our daughter clambered over to me. She tripped over her feet, and I caught her. "I've got you, sweetheart. I have you, Jade." I tried out the name we'd picked out for her.

Her head tipped in response. She blinked up at me with her bright green eyes.

"She likes it."

Raphael held out his hands. "Well, Sage? What do you think?"

Sage flapped his little wings, unfurling them from his body, then he leapt into Raphael's arms.

I laughed. "I think he likes his name too."

Now that they were hatched, we would have to let our pack know. Theo would be coming over so that he could properly introduce himself to his new niece and nephew. Plus, Alpha Tyler would want to get a good look at his two newest pack members.

Soon, we would text pictures and a proper birth announcement to Raphael's brothers, each of which had found their own mates and had clutches of their own.

I smiled at my mate. The two of us sat side by side. He held our son while I held our daughter. The two of them looked at one another and let out sharp chirps of excitement.

I laughed. "They recognize each other."

"They do. They are so perfect, mate." Eventually, they would shift to their human form and stay that way for a while, but for now, I was going to get as much dragon snuggle time as I could.

I laid my head on Raphael's shoulder. "I love you so much, my mate."

His dragon hummed with delight. "And I love you, Luca."

Bonus Epilogue

Raphael

Six Months Later

Luca fastened our daughter into her car seat while I tucked Sage's toy next to him. At six months old, he could grasp his little stuffed dragon with the ferociousness of a dragon protecting his hoard, and scales forbid if we ever left home without it. He did not do well when his dragon wasn't near.

Jade didn't have an attachment to any toys, but she sure didn't like it when she lost sight of someone. It didn't matter who it was, as long as she could see someone, she was happy. Which was why we had a picture of all of us on the back of the seat so she could see it from her car seat.

"Do we have everything?" Luca asked.

"Yup. Cooler is all packed with the food, and the gifts are stuffed in the back."

"Okay." Luca stood outside the car, clearly lost in thought, going over the mental list of the things we needed for our short trip. This would be the first time we had gone anywhere with the children overnight, and it had taken weeks of preparation to make it possible.

The stars had somehow aligned, and we would be visiting my brothers and their mates after all this time. Brock and his mate were hosting a barbeque. Luca and I had three days off, and we planned on making a mini vacation out of it. Of course, it had taken tons of coordination and a whole SUV stuffed full of supplies in order to make it happen.

"Okay. I think we have everything." Luca climbed into the passenger seat while I took position behind the wheel.

I grinned as we set off down the road. Sage and Jade happily babbled to each other as we drove. They couldn't see one another, but as long as they could hear each other coo and gibber, they were happy. Much like when they had been in their shells, the two of them had a language all their own. Heaven help us when the two of them were mobile and could really get into mischief. Already we had thought about keeping them in separate rooms since they would wake each other up in the middle of the night just to chat with one another.

"I can't believe we're finally going to meet the rest of the family." Luca reached over and held my hand.

We had done video calls with my brothers, their mates, and their kids. We shared pictures and sought each other out for advice on raising young dragons, but we hadn't seen each other in person in a long time.

Luca embraced my brothers and their mates like long-lost siblings, despite having never met them in person. "I know. I can't wait to see all the little ones." It was crazy how many children there were between the three of us. Our two would have more cousins than they could name, and I loved it.

"What if they don't like their gifts?" Luca asked.

I snorted out a laugh. "The kids are the same age as ours. I'm pretty sure they will be more enamored with the shiny paper the gifts are wrapped in rather than the gifts themselves, mate. But in time, they will love them immensely."

"It isn't a silly gift?" Luca chewed his thumbnail like he did when he was nervous.

I grabbed his hand and held it.

Luca and I had debated on what sorts of gifts to get our nieces and nephews. Not that we were expected to come bearing gifts, but we wanted to.

In the end we'd opted to get tiny treasure chests made for them, big enough to be used as the start of their hoards when it came time for them. Perhaps it was an impractical gift for small children, but in time, they would appreciate the significance of it.

Also, my brothers each insisted on no toys. Much like Luca and I had. We were drowning in toys at the house, and the little ones could barely play with them yet!

"Are we there yet?" Luca asked after only twenty minutes.

I laughed, lifting his hand to my lips and kissing his knuckles. "Not quite, love. Patience."

"I can't help it! I'm too excited!"

I grinned. My mate couldn't be more perfect. "I am too, love. I am too."

Life couldn't get any more perfect.

Next In Series

Nesting Ever After Season Two

Marked By His Alpha Dragon's Desire by Jena Wade

Claimed by His Dragon Omega's Fire by Toby Wise

Alpha Dragon's Wings of Love by Lorelei M. Hart

Find the other dragon adventures in the Nesting Ever After Season One shared world!

The Sapphire Dragon's Missing Mate by Lorelei M. Hart
The Amethyst Dragon's Mythical Mate by Toby Wise

Also By Jena Wade

Fire Wings

The Emerald Dragon's Moonlit Mate

Naughty Elf: Shimmersnap

My Omega's Miracle

Royals Of Swena

The Prince's Blind Date

The Prince's Bodyguard

The Prince's Husband

The Prince's Barista

The Prince's Teacher

Windridge Den

Desired Bear (with Lorelei M. Hart)

Chased Bear (with Lorelei M. Hart)

Destined Bear (with Lorelei M. Hart)

Mated In The Mafia

Omega for the Mafia Boss (with Aria Grace)
Forbidden Omega (with Aria Grace)
Undercover Mafia Alpha (with Aria Grace)
Bought By the Mafia Alpha (with Aria Grace)
Bound to the Mafia Guard (with Aria Grace)
Mafia's Broken Omega (with Aria Grace)
Mafia Heir's Alpha (with Aria Grace)

Centaurs

The Centaur's Secret (with Lorelei M. Hart)

The Centaur's Sacrifice (with Lorelei M. Hart)

The Centaur's Spell(with Lorelei. M. Hart)

Asilo Pride

His Damaged Pride (with Lorelei M. Hart)

His Damaged Pack(with Lorelei M. Hart)

His Damaged Mate(with Lorelei M. Hart)

His Damaged Beast (with Lorelei M. Hart)

His Damaged Purpose (with Lorelei M. Hart)

His Damaged Fate (with Lorelei M. Hart)

Fractured Fang

Alpha (with Lorelei M. Hart)

Beta (with Lorelei M. Hart)

Omega (with Lorelei M. Hart)

Steelwick Pride

Protecing His Pride (with Lorelei M. Hart)

Protecting His Purpose (with Lorelei M. Hart)

Protecting His Potential(with Lorelei M. Hart)

Protecting His Passion (with Lorelei M. Hart)

Northbay Pack

Claiming His Pack (with Lorelei M. Hart)

Claiming His Purpose (with Lorelei M. Hart)

Claiming His Potential (with Lorelei M. Hart)

Claiming His Passion (with Lorelei M. Hart)

Greycoast Pack

Finding His Pack (with Lorelei M. Hart)

Finding His Purpose (with Lorelei M. Hart)

Finding His Potential (with Lorelei M. Hart)

Finding His Passion (with Lorelei M. Hart)

The Greycoast Pack: The Complete Collection

The Greycoast Pack: The Shorts

Daddy Wolf (with Victoria Sue)

Contemporary

Caught

A Little Christmas: Oscar's Secret

His Cowboy

Jump to Recipe

Royals Of Swena

The Prince's Blind Date

The Prince's Bodyguard

The Prince's Husband

The Prince's Barista

The Prince's Teacher

Lights of Fate

Blue

Purple

Orange

Bake Sale Bachelors

Sugar Cookie Kisses

Apple Pie Pair

Mint Chocolate Mayhem

Blueberry Pie Beau

Salted Caramel Chaos

Red Velvet Regret

Rocky Road Rendezvous

Tall Tails

Unexpected Packages

Rochdale Security

The Bodyguard's Charge

The Bodyguard's Relationship

The Bodyguard's Professor (with Lorelei M. Hart)

The Bodyguard's Assistant

The Bodyguard's Technician (with Lorelei M. Hart)

The Bodyguard's Christmas Surprise

Rochdale Security Boxset

Millerstown Moments

Dashboard Lights

All Revved Up

Crying Out Loud (with Lorelei M. Hart)

Anything For Love

Life is a Lemon (with Lorelei M. Hart)

Millerstown Moments Boxset

Heaven Can Wait

Vale Valley

Picture Purrfect

The Cat & The Hound

Dragons

Dragon's Fire

Dragon's Ice

Dragon's Stone

Dragon's Jewel

Dragon's Spark

Dragon's Boxset

Directions

Up to Code

Down to Earth

Back to You

Directions Boxset

Shorts

Alpha Student

Alpha Doctor

Season of Hope

About Jena Wade

Subscribe to my Newsletter to get the latest info! (I promise not to spam)

I live in Michigan with my husband, two dogs, and three children. By day I work as a software developer and at night I write. I was born and raised on a farm and I spend most of my free time outdoors, playing in the garden or tending to my landscaping.

***

I like my books sweet, sexy and full of romance. I love to hear from my readers and would be more than happy to answer any questions you may have about my work! Feel free to email me at thejenawade@gmail.com.

In the meantime, visit me on Amazon.

Printed in Dunstable, United Kingdom

66349106R00080